COLD HEARTED

NICOLE HOUSTON

Published by *Urban Rose Publishing*
Cover Design by *Aleksandar Novovic*
Editor: *Emily Fuggetta*

Join Nicole Houston's Newsletter

Follow Nicole Houston

http://urbanrosepublishing.com

My Brother's Wife

TABLE OF CONTENTS

CHAPTER 1

I looked around and realized we were heading along a different path. My best friend, Riane, and the rest of the medical team members were quiet and obviously anxious about what was happening.

This was not the scene we were expecting when we eagerly volunteered for this medical mission. Our destination was supposed to be the military camp in the East—not the heart of Sylvania Mountain where these rebels probably dwelled.

"This is it, we're gonna die," Riane whispered in terror, cautious lest our abductors would hear her.

I held her hand and squeezed it tightly. "Don't say that," I said, trying to console her, although a part of me was also terrified about what was going to happen.

"Move faster!" one of the rebels yelled impatiently when our colleagues, Phil and Lily, came to a halt for a quick rest.

"What have we done wrong to deserve this, Aiya?" Riane said again, just loud enough for me to hear. "We just want to give some aid and serve the country," she added, full of remorse. "I should have listened to my mum."

Was Phil having the same regret in his mind? I couldn't look him in the eye. I was the one who'd convinced him and his family to sign up and join us. If it wasn't for me, he wouldn't be here at all. He would probably be spending some quality time with his wife and kids.

"Shhh… calm down. We're going to be alright, trust me," I replied, but my attention was focused on Phil and Lily now, who looked as frightened as Riane was.

The rebel was about to give Phil a blow to the stomach, so I tried to distract him.

"Can't we have a rest for a while? We're so tired already! We've been walking for hours!" I yelled at him.

He turned to me as the rest of his pals chuckled in delight—as if they longed to witness a great show that would somehow make their day a little more interesting. He drew his gun and approached me. His eyes were dangerous and threatening, and it was giving me a chill inside. I swallowed, trying to keep my composure.

"I. Don't. Give. A. Fuck," he answered, emphasizing each word. Then, he dragged me away from Riane angrily. "Why don't you lead your friends instead?" he hissed, sarcastic.

"But they're exhausted!" I protested, staring anxiously at my friends, especially Phil, who seemed to be catching his breath now. He was a bit overweight and was not used to a long trek like this.

"It's okay, Aiya," Phil called after me, apologetic. "We can still walk," he assured me, but he was still struggling from keeping up with us.

I closed my eyes, feeling sorry for us.

How are we going to survive this? Is the military aware now that we were abducted by their enemies?

I sighed deeply and stepped forward, following the taller one who was leading the way. At the same time, I took advantage of every moment, trying to familiarize myself with their faces just in case. There were seven people escorting us, but only three of them had the guts to show their faces, and it was obvious a few were undressing me with their eyes—one in particular.

"I think I already know what's on your mind, Hunter," the tall one said.

So, his name is Hunter.

The man chuckled maliciously but didn't say anything.

"Let's see… brown-skinned, curly hair, curvy body. She is exactly the type of girl you like to bang!" the tall one said again, and I knew by then where their conversation was going.

Someone, please save us! I thought, cringing as their private joke squirmed in my head like a nightmare starting to take root in the deepest part of me. I must not cry. I must stay optimistic for the sake of everyone.

"Cut it out, Joe," Hunter snapped, but his eyes were gleaming with desire. "I don't want any one of you to stress her out for the moment. She has to be in the mood when we get there."

All of them laughed loudly, completely delighted as they realized they were terrifying me.

"What do you want from us?" Riane asked all of a sudden. Her voice was trembling, and tears were starting to invade her eyes.

"Nothing, really," Joe answered, full of malice. "We just wanted some new company," he added as their laughter roared around us.

✳ ✳ ✳

Finally, we reached the heart of the mountain where the rebels resided. It was obvious that they had lived in the area for a long time. If I was not mistaken, there were more than fifty of them, and they were armed, making me wonder where they got all those weapons.

We were led to a large cell that looked more like a barn. Everybody on the medical team was tied up except for me and Phil, who were taken away from our colleagues.

"Wait!" Phil gasped, still looking tired, thirsty and starving.

Lily and Riane shouted in distress as they took us away.

I couldn't muster a word of protest. I was too exhausted, and I knew I should save up all my remaining strength to think of ways to escape this unfortunate incarceration.

As we were taken away, I heard Lily and Riane's voices cry out in protest, but it wasn't helping. Their shrieks faded away as we came across a group of men in one corner who seemed to be having a good time, drinks in hand.

"Hey, Joe!" one of them shouted with a wild grin at the man who was clasping my arm. "Where are you taking her?"

"Don't take it the wrong way, guys. Hunter needs her tonight," he replied with a grin of his own.

"What about that big guy over there? He needs him, too?" the man asked, a little confounded as he saw how the others were dragging Phil behind us.

"Nah," Joe said. "The fishes need bigger and healthier bait. He'll be of great use." He laughed loudly, leaving Phil and me completely mortified.

What does he mean? I thought, anxious.

I was brought to one of the huts, the biggest and most secluded one. When the door was opened, Hunter's familiar and menacing face greeted me and Joe.

"Hi, baby," he said and grinned. "Come in."

It was then I realized Phil and his escorts were not with us anymore.

"Where's Phil?" I asked. My voice was a little shaky, but I managed to regain my composure just before I was ushered inside the shack. "What will you do to him?" I asked, more firmly now, and turned my attention to Hunter, who obviously possessed the real authority in the group.

Hunter stared at me in awe. "That's the spirit! I like it!" he exclaimed and took in my scent like a hungry wolf. "You still smell nice, you know," he added and snatched at my hair crazily.

I moved back a few steps away from him. Surprisingly, he let my hair go. I was expecting the action to piss him off, but he looked more amused than offended, which made me feel a little relieved.

For a moment, he paid attention to Joe. He nodded to him and gave him a signal to leave us alone. All of a sudden, my whole body turned cold and numb. I wanted to scream for help, but I knew it would be a useless stunt.

"Where is Phil?" I asked him again as soon as he closed the door and turned his attention back to me. "What did you do to him?"

"You keep asking about him, honey," he said and narrowed his eyes. "You're making me feel jealous." He sat me down and stared at my whole body for quite a long time.

"Just tell me where he is, then I'll keep my mouth shut," I replied, completely attentive to his every move now. *If he makes one bad move, I am going to kick his dick so hard it will make him kneel in pain.*

Hunter stood at the window, and then his lunatic expression suddenly morphed into one chillingly severe.

"Your friends… especially that big guy you were asking about? They will be safe here… unharmed… untouched…" he whispered. "But it will all depend on your performance, my dear," he continued with a smirk.

Performance?

Hunter glared at me meaningfully, and every bit of my soul cringed in horror. I could see in his eyes he wanted me to do him an extraordinary favor. I could see that it was something that would ruin my whole life. What did he want from me? Did he want me to please him?

Oh, no! Dear Lord! Help me!

"As much as I wanted to have you right now, I must preserve you for a greater purpose," Hunter said. His voice was serious, but his eyes were dark.

"W-what do you mean?" I mumbled, trying to dig another dose of remaining courage out of my chest.

Hunter pulled out a small bottle from his pocket. He showed it to me carefully.

"We're going to have a deal, baby," he said, smirking. "I will let you go alone while your friends stay with us for a while. You'll head straight to the military camp, tell them you've escaped, and somehow, I need you to gain their trust. Befriend the cooks if you must, I don't really care how the hell you do it! I just need you to put this poison in their meal… it's very simple, isn't it?"

I was confused, and it took a while before I finally absorbed his instruction. He wanted me to mass poison the soldiers in exchange for my friends' freedom. Riane, Lily and Phil's faces suddenly flashed in my head. I wanted to cry, but I had to keep my composure.

"No," I answered firmly. "Just kill me if you must."

"Ooh…" Hunter said, circling me theatrically. "I'd rather not," he continued. "Besides, you have no other choice, Miss Shaw. I don't usually take 'no' for an answer."

Just as I was absorbing the situation, we heard gunshots from nearby. Hunter moved away from me and surveyed the surrounding area through a small hole in the wall.

"Damn!" he exclaimed angrily as he turned in my direction. The door suddenly burst open. Hunter was too quick, jumping out of the window, leaving me scared and confused with the strangers who busted in.

"Don't move!" one of them pointed his gun at me for a moment, but when he realized I was tied up, he put it down immediately. "What's your name?" the stranger asked while his buddies moved around the shack to survey the place.

"Aiyana Shaw," I answered, almost choking.

"Ah! Miss Shaw!" he uttered as if we were already acquainted with each other. "I'm Lieutenant Allen Blake. It's okay now. We're going to get you out of here!" He quickly managed to free me from the rope around my wrists.

"Oh, thank goodness!" I exclaimed in relief. "They're keeping the others in the barn," I told him without a trace of fear now. "And Phil! They took him away from us!" I added as I remembered my pal.

"We got them already, don't worry. Only the two of you were missing from our list," he informed me.

"Sir! He escaped!" one of the men said.

"Go and find him!" Allen ordered firmly at the same time, ushering me out of the hut with one hand on my arm. "Now, we only need to find Phil!" he whispered urgently. Then, he called over his radio, asking around if everyone was marked safe. Still, no Phil.

The sound of trading gunfire was something I would always remember for sure. Although we were being rescued now, a part of me was still wondering if we would be able to make it out safely.

We reached a large tree a few meters away from the hideout. It was then I caught a glimpse of Lily and Riane. They ran towards me and hugged me in tears as we took refuge on the overlarge roots of the wild tree.

"Oh, Aiya! Thank God!" Riane cried and embraced me tightly as if we hadn't seen each other for years.

I couldn't tell how many soldiers were scattered around the tree, but I was completely certain we were being protected by an assigned military team which probably included the soldier named Allen Blake.

"Is everyone okay?" he asked, panting, his eyes surveying around for any sign of danger.

"Yes," Riane answered promptly, wiping the tears from her eyes and letting me go for the first time.

Allen spoke over the radio. "We got the three roses. The three roses are safe, I repeat, the three roses are safe!" he called out.

"Copy that," said a voice from the other end. "How about the leaf?"

"Still negative," Allen responded, a little disappointed.

"Find the leaf! Find the leaf! We will cover you!" the voice commanded. It was a very authoritative, masculine voice. Something I'd find sexy if only we were not in the middle of an encounter.

"Yes, sir!"

I assumed they were talking about us—the girls were the roses, and Phil was the leaf.

✳ ✳ ✳

The nerve-wracking gunshots subsided a little, a sign that the battle was almost over. There were a few casualties from the rebel group already. I had no idea if there were casualties from the soldiers because as far as I could see, none of the dead bodies in the area wore a military uniform, and I hoped I was correct.

"We're leaving! We have to take you out of here!" Allen informed us and the rest of the team protecting us.

"But what about Phil?!" I protested. "We can't leave him!"

Allen came to me, assuring me that it would be alright. "The other group will search for him, okay? Now, please, we need to get you out of here safely," he said.

I didn't say anything more. They knew better than me, and I needed to cooperate with them. So, we ran as fast as we could with the rest of the soldiers circling us.

I held Lily's hand and reached for Riane's, as well. But as I looked around, I realized she was not with us anymore.

"Riane? Riane!" I yelled, feeling restless. It was dark already. The tall trees and the bushes were not helping to figure out if she was still with us or not.

Everybody halted. Allen came to me and covered my mouth.

15

"Shhh…" he whispered.

And we all kept quiet, trying to listen. The battle noises could be heard from a distance now, indicating that we'd managed to escape from the deadly scene.

"Help! Help!" I heard Riane's voice. She was still close.

"They got her!" I yelled in panic, and Lily mumbled a prayer as her whole body was shaking in fear.

"Oh, God! Please… no!" she cried, her hands on her chest. We embraced each other, desperately listening. Some escorts left us as Allen instructed them to search around for Riane.

"PLEASE! HELP ME!"

Riane's voice echoed in the woods, and I was absolutely certain it was coming from the west side.

"It's coming from over there! She's over there!" I insisted to the soldiers who kept running in the wrong direction. I looked at Allen, who was leading the command, but he was on the radio, reporting to whoever the person on the other end of the line was.

Impatient and feeling absolutely frustrated at the incompetence, I let go of Lily and ran in the right direction myself, hearing the terrified scream of my friend.

"No! Aiyana! Don't!" Lily begged, but it was too late. All I had in mind now was to save my best friend.

"Damn!" Allen's voice echoed behind, but my attention was focused on where Riane was. One quick distraction and we might lose her whereabouts.

"RIANE?!" I yelled with the loudest voice I could ever muster. "RIANE! WHERE ARE YOU?!"

She shrieked, and I could tell I was getting close. I doubled my effort, passing trees and bushes at a surprising speed. Finally, I saw her, trying to fight with all her might against the perpetrator who was dragging her away.

"Riane!" I shouted, distracting the bandit. He had a gun pointed at my friend's head.

"Don't move! Or else, I'll shoot her!" the rebel said, desperately keeping his composure as Riane was struggling from his hold.

"Let her go!" I said.

"Stay back!" the guy warned, but my adrenaline kept rushing through my veins, pushing me to grab my friend at any cost.

Riane was terrified. It was all over her face. She was sweating madly, and it seemed like she was losing her strength now. I stepped forward, feeling no fear at all. I couldn't let anything distract me in that moment.

I need to save her!

Luckily, the rebel lost his balance as he stepped on what looked like a slippery old trunk. I was able to snatch Riane's arm as soon as he fell on the ground. Then, I heard him hit something, making him a little disoriented.

"Fuck!" he growled angrily.

I pushed my best friend towards the right path in the woods. We ran, struggling but determined to escape. I was not so sure if the man was able to get back on his feet again, but a loud gunshot came from his direction.

Did someone shoot him from somewhere, or did he shoot someone else?

And then, after a few more seconds, I felt my body go numb as I gradually lost my balance. I fell down and felt my leg break, but

I couldn't scream in pain anymore. My whole consciousness was being dragged away from reality.

I stumbled helplessly and saw Riane's frightened expression as she rushed towards me on the ground. It was then that I realized that I was the one who had been shot. I could sense the gushes of blood coming from my left shoulder.

"Aiya!" Riane cried, my blood dyeing her already messy white shirt. "Stay with me, okay? Stay with me!" she mumbled, and her hands were cold and shaking.

Then, there were multiple gunshots everywhere, but I couldn't see anymore.

"W-what's happening?" I asked her weakly.

Riane was sobbing as I felt her trying to give me the proper first aid for a gunshot wound. I had no idea if it was something serious; I could not feel anything. "Don't worry, they got him. He's dead. We're safe," she whispered to me reassuringly, but her tone revealed her absolute distress.

CHAPTER 2

Aiya, wake up!

Immediately, I opened my eyes. Riane's terrified voice was still echoing in my head, and my conscious self was debating if that particular scenario was true or just part of a bad dream.

I stared at the ceiling as I tried to recall what was happening. Looking around, the unfamiliar room finally alerted me that it was not just a nightmare after all. Everything that I and the other medical team members had experienced was definitely real. We had been captured by the rebels and rescued by the military.

"Phil!" I uttered as I remembered him. *Did they find him?* I wondered. I got up and an unbearable pain suddenly coursed through me. I was all alone and in panic. *What happened?*

I calmed myself, and soon enough everything made sense. I was shot, and I was treated here. So, I lay back, adjusting to the bandage on my shoulder and casted broken leg.

"Jeez, this hurt more than I expected!" I mumbled to myself, hoping someone would finally burst in the room to explain everything to me. I could not wait to hear the story. I wanted to believe that everyone was safe.

I remained silent for a few more minutes that felt like forever. Gladly, I heard footsteps. I waited, and to my relief, Riane appeared, her face peaceful and appeased, indicating that there was no more danger.

"Aiya!" she exclaimed happily and rushed towards me. She had a small bandage around her left arm, but she seemed to have fully recovered.

She hugged me gently. "Finally, you woke up! Oh, we were so worried!"

✶ ✶ ✶

I was checked by the head nurse, Sandra, before she left me and Riane alone again.

My best friend ended up in tears as she recalled the whole thing. She was so grateful that I had chased them, and although I kept insisting that I hadn't really done anything, she insisted that I was the one who rescued her from death.

"I can't believe you'd really risk your life for me, Aiya," she said seriously.

"Of course, I would," I said, but my voice was still a little weak since the gush of pain would strike all over my body as I talked and moved. "You're my best friend. I know you would do the same for me."

She just gave me a smile and squeezed my hand tenderly. "Hey, I better get going. It's late, you need to rest," she said.

"But can't you stay a little bit? I'm not sleepy yet," I requested, theatrically pouting my lips like a child.

Riane sighed sympathetically. "I would love to, girl," she said. "But Commander Blake will surely get angry again if he finds me here at this hour."

"Commander Blake? Is that the one who accompanied us? Allen Blake?" I wondered.

"Nope, that's his brother. I was talking about Commander Tristan Blake, the rude one," she whispered. "Gosh, I hate him. He is so arrogant. You know, he hates you."

"Hates *me*? I haven't met him yet, so how come?" I asked defensively.

"Well, he just doesn't like how you pursued me and my abductor. He said you messed up the rescue plan," Riane explained.

"By coming after you? What the heck?" I mumbled, feeling a bit irritated. They should have been thanking me. His team had gone in the wrong direction. It was so unfair.

Riane stood up and gave me a kiss on my cheek. "I'll go ahead now. We'll talk more, tomorrow, okay? It's time for me to go," she added and hurried out before I could ask her what was on my mind.

"Wait… how about Phil? Did they find him?" I called out, but nobody answered back.

✶ ✶ ✶

It was probably midnight, and I could sense some people roaming around the hall, probably surveying the whole camp. As much as I wanted to doze off, still, I could not fall asleep. My wound on my shoulder was hurting so bad, it was quite excruciating. I was so helpless, I couldn't even move my feet.

So, I waited for another minute or so, trying to ease every ache in my body. For sure, someone from the medical staff would come to do one more round to check me on. But to my dismay, there was no sign of a doctor or nurse to see if I was still okay or not.

I could feel I was getting a fever now. My bones were aching, as well, and I really needed to take a painkiller.

"Hello?" I said, hoping someone out there would hear me. "Is anybody there?"

However, all I could hear back was the echo of my own voice.

It was cold, but I was sweating madly. I was feeling really ill now. So, I looked around, and soon, I realized there were some pills placed on my bedside table.

There must be something there, I thought.

So, without thinking, I tried to reach the painkillers. But I had overestimated my ability to maneuver around to self-medicate, and before I knew it, I was crumpled on the floor as my injured body burned like crazy.

"Aww…" I cried discreetly, but the shattering medicine bottles and containers fell down with me and created a very alarming noise.

A short while later, there were footsteps entering the room.

"Oh, dear! What happened to you?" Sandra's familiar voice asked worriedly.

I looked up, tears blinding my eyes. By now, I was shivering, the pain in my leg was too much to bear, and I wasn't so sure if I would be able to explain myself without stuttering.

"I-I'm sorry… I was just trying to reach the painkillers," I tried to explain, trying to clear my eyesight.

"You should have called me," she said with concern.

I did, I protested silently.

"Just as stubborn as she is," said a guy's voice with a cold tone.

Then, I heard Allen. "Come on, she's hurt," he commented.

Then, I felt someone was trying to reach me. Relieved, he lifted me back onto my bed and settled me very cautiously. He smelled so good. His hard and broad chest was something I could not ignore, and his breathing, although it sounded harsh and hostile, filled my stomach with butterflies.

"T-thanks, that feels better," I told him appreciatively.

But the guy who carried me sneered in disapproval while Sandra came back to me with a tablet and a glass of water.

"Here, take this, honey," she said. Pacified, I took it very gratefully.

"Thanks so much," I said.

"Are you feeling better now?" Allen inquired after a few minutes while Sandra was cleaning up the mess scattered on the floor.

"You should at least be careful about moving, Miss Shaw," the guy with a cold tone of voice cut in. He was the same guy who'd carried me back to bed. He was tall, blue-eyed, white and rosy-cheeked and had a more masculine build than Lieutenant Allen. It was hard for me to figure out if his hair was blonde because he was wearing a military cap, but I suspected he was.

"Oh, this is Commander Tristan Blake," Sandra said and dashed back, embarrassed at how she'd forgotten to introduce him to me.

So, this is the rude one Riane was talking about.

"..and this is Lieutenant Allen Blake, by the way," Sandra continued.

"Yes, we have met already at the rescue, Sandra," Allen informed her kindly and grinned, revealing his dimples on both cheeks. He was really good-looking with a genuine personality. He resembled his brother, except for the square face and cleft chin, and Commander Tristan Blake was probably two inches taller than him. Allen's consistent friendly smile and tone of voice were making him distinct and likeable compared to his sexy, handsome but grumpy-looking brother.

Before I could even answer, Tristan cut in again, ignoring the friendly mood that his brother was trying to build.

"Miss Shaw, may I remind you that you came here to volunteer as a nurse, to aid my soldiers and not to become one of the patients?" Tristan said.

"Yeah, I know that, sir," I answered, feeling a little offended. His rudeness was dousing all the dreamy thoughts in my head. I already knew where he was heading.

"Well, I am so glad to hear it. Perhaps, it will remind you not to act impulsively all the time. Last time, you got yourself shot because you ran to help your friend, unarmed. Now, you are creating another opportunity to harm yourself and to cause another inconvenience to everyone," Commander Blake uttered with a poker face.

My heart was in a sudden fury. I wanted to shout in his face and tell him how terrible I was feeling in that moment. I hoped he would consider that before scolding me like a guilty child. But he was the commander, so I said nothing to pay respect and kept all the protests inside my head instead.

CHAPTER 3

The next morning, I woke up late and saw that Lily was the one in charge of me. She cleaned my wounds and finally gave me my morning medicines. Although she was relieved of our safety, it was she who informed me that Phil was still missing.

"I hope and pray that he's still alive," she whispered anxiously but obviously trying to sound a little optimistic in front of me.

"Don't worry, he will be fine. They will find him soon," I assured her, but a twinge of pain and anxiety wrapped up my senses as I felt the gravity of our situation. His safety depended not just on the military alone. It depended on me.

When Lily left, I cried silent tears. I was still confused, and I hoped I could undo everything. I had asked him to join the volunteer group, and it had put his life in danger.

Suddenly, a soft knock interrupted my quiet turmoil, and when I looked up, Allen was standing at the entrance, his handsome brown eyes greeting me pleasantly.

"Good morning," he said, a little hesitant as he probably saw me not in a good mood at all. "Are you okay? Do you need help?" he asked, a little worried.

"No, I'm fine," I lied. "C-can I help you?" I wondered, discreetly schooling my features so that he couldn't see my emotional turmoil.

"Oh, I just thought you might need this to cheer you up and help you get better," he said and showed me a stem of a beautiful large flower I hadn't ever seen before.

It was as if my heart suddenly melted at the sight of the flower. It looked like a large rose in deep pink, but I was sure I'd never laid my eyes on its beauty before. Suddenly, my mood swung to a totally different one. It gave me a lighter feeling as if it was boosting the last remaining happiness deep within my soul.

"Wow, that's so beautiful," I uttered in awe. "What kind of flower is that?" I asked him.

"It's a *middlemist*," he answered, revealing his dimples. "It's one of the rarest species, by the way," he told me confidently.

"Really? And you got one here on the battlefield?" I chuckled, a little sarcastic and overwhelmed.

"Yeah, who would ever think it blooms here, right?" he said. "Now, where should we put it?"

Looking around, he placed the stem at the bedside and went out the door for a minute or so. I waited momentarily, wondering what he was up to. When he came back, he had a glass of water in his hand and put in the stem in it.

"That will do," he commented proudly, and then he looked at me. "We always improvise a lot of stuff here," he added and winked.

"I can see that," I said and grinned, thankful that somehow, someone from the military was treating me nicely. "Thanks."

"Not a big deal," he replied.

"Well, it means a lot to me. And of course, thanks for saving us from the rebels! That was a big deal. Thanks for coming for us," I continued.

"That one, it was part of our duty," he answered and occupied the stool beside the bed as he surveyed me. "It was a group effort."

"How're your wounds?" he asked.

"A little better," I replied.

"Do you remember what you did in the field? Damn, you were such a badass back there!" he commented, smirking wildly at me. "It pissed off our commander!" He clearly found the thought amusing.

I blushed, feeling totally embarrassed as I remembered how I'd acted like a bulletproof superhero. "I'm so sorry... I was so impulsive..." I said, covering my face with my hand.

"Of course, I couldn't blame you. I would do the same if I was in your shoes. My team was running the wrong way, anyway. So, you had every right to do so... whatever was on your mind back then," he said and laughed again.

I chuckled with him for a moment. Somehow, I forgot my current dilemma. "But seriously, did I really cause a lot of trouble to your team?"

"*Ugh*," Allen uttered. "We have faced much worse trouble compared to that. Don't listen to my brother, he is quite a pain in the ass to almost everyone around here. He always talks harshly. Such a heartless soul, everyone says that."

"R-really? Is he really a heartless one?" I wondered.

"I really can't tell, though. Maybe, he's just under stress. The pressure is always on him because he handles a very serious job. When we planned the rescue, he was aiming for zero casualties and zero injuries on our side. Well, luckily, nobody from our side was killed. Perhaps, he was just a little frustrated because you got severely injured and your colleague was still left missing," he explained.

✶ ✶ ✶

A few days after I was discharged from the confinement, I made sure I was able to fulfill my duty diligently as a medical staff in the camp. I should say that my first week as a volunteer was a bit tough because I could see how Commander Tristan Blake hated my presence.

But his brother was a big help for me. I was starting to win the confidence and trust of the soldiers in the camp because of him. There were times he and their marching platoon would chant their morning greetings to me as soon as I would trace my course to the camp's clinic in the morning.

"I think he's into you," Riane whispered while we were having our coffee break.

"Who?" I asked, surprised.

"Come on, you should know by now, Aiya!" she exclaimed, rolling her eyes in disbelief. "I'm talking about Lieutenant Allen," she added.

I blushed, a little intrigued. *Is he?*

"Well, he's cute," I commented, trying to give my best friend a taste of conversation she likes.

"Come on, he's not just cute. He's perfectly nice and handsome!" she corrected dreamily as if she was imagining a fairy tale prince, a warrior riding a majestic and beautiful white horse.

"I could sense how you like him," I said, chuckling. "Don't worry, he's all yours," I continued.

"Yeah, I like him, but I think he likes you. So, I'm not going to intervene," Riane answered and laughed.

"That's very generous of you," I replied and snickered.

"Anything for you," she responded with a wink.

"But seriously, that's not my priority right now," I assured her, and suddenly my thoughts reminded me of Phil, who needed to be rescued as soon as possible. *I have to ask Lieutenant Allen for an update.*

"His brother was much hotter, though," Riane said all of a sudden.

"You mean, Commander Tristan Blake?" I inquired.

"Who else?" Riane said, rolling her eyes. "But Tristan Blake is not the type of guy we would date," she commented.

Yeah, she's right. Commander Tristan was gorgeous but very snobbish and moody. Somehow, I felt disappointed that he hated me, but I wasn't sure why.

✶ ✶ ✶

"Aiyana, would you please proceed to the meeting room?" Sandra asked, looking a little exhausted. "I'm sorry, I know you're just about to have your lunch. But no one else is available right now, and you're the only one I can trust on this one," she added.

I had no idea if she was just trying to flatter me or something, but if she really needed a hand, I was more than willing to help.

"Sure, Miss Sandra, no worries," I replied and brought back my belongings to the locker room. "How can I help?"

"The captain got a minor cut on his hand while they were having a closed-door meeting," she said.

"How?" I asked, curious.

"Well, he, unfortunately, dropped the glass in his hand and tried to pick up the broken pieces on the floor," she explained, her face a little apathetic at the thought.

I chuckled a little, trying to catch the hidden humor she was trying to convey. "If it's not life-threatening, I think I can handle it," I said and winked.

"Thanks a lot," she said and handed me the supplies I would need to clean and cover the cut.

✶ ✶ ✶

Before I headed to the meeting room, Sandra reminded me that aside from the captain, almost everybody was present in the place including Commander Tristan Blake. She knew how he hated me from head to toe. In fact, she told me how he was accusing me of flirting with everybody.

I cleared away the negative thoughts in my head as soon as I reached the office door. The two soldier guards nodded at me kindly, and then one of them knocked twice, informing those who were inside the hall of my presence.

"Finally!" the head of the troop said, acknowledging my arrival. He seemed old, but still in good shape. Her gray hair and dark skin obviously showed a trail of his experiences on the battlefield. "What a beautiful young lady we have here," the captain said while clutching his palm soaked in blood.

"Good morning, captain," I said, clearing my throat. "Miss Sandra sent me here," I added as if I was trying to justify my presence to Tristan alone because he seemed very unfriendly with his accusing stare. His intense glare was making me a bit uncomfortable.

"Of course," the captain responded. "I could use some help here," he added and showed me his injury. So, without further ado, I approached him and started cleaning his cut.

Indeed, it was just a minor laceration. I was able to do the job quickly. After putting on the bandage, I told him everything was set, and the captain complimented my work appreciatively.

"Thanks, Miss Shaw," he said. "I feel better now, you did a great job. But I think I'd be willing to get more cuts just so I can see you more often," he continued, kidding.

✷ ✷ ✷

Finally, I could get some sleep! I wolfed down my lunch and made my way back to our lounge. I had been awake for almost twenty-four hours now on duty, and my body was begging for some sleep.

As I walked through the corridor, Commander Tristan suddenly exited from the meeting room. I tried my best to ignore the awkward situation, hoping he would turn in the other direction. However, he was heading the same way I was, and obviously there was no way I could back out. He already saw me walking right towards him.

He halted just as I reached him, leaving me no choice but to greet him.

"Good morning, sir," I said, trying my best to sound as casual as possible. I gave him a smile as he caught my stare, and I honestly expected him to greet me back.

"Really? Are you trying to use your charm on me now, Miss Shaw?" he asked, sarcastic.

What? What's wrong with him? I'm just trying to be nice!

I didn't respond. I tried to hold my emotion as his words flared up my whole being. My subconscious was protesting, pushing me to defend myself against him for once.

Come on! You've been awake for hours! You're so tired! You don't deserve this maltreatment!

"Speechless?" Tristan uttered, waking up my whole defensive soul. "I always believe that silence means 'yes.' Let me tell you this, it may work on everybody in the camp, which includes our boss, but it will never work on me. You should take note of that," he said and walked away proudly.

I could not contain my fury. He was out of line. I wasn't even getting paid for this medical mission. He had no right to accuse me of something I'd never done at all. If he only knew what I'd been going through. If only he knew how Hunter was forcing me to choose between them and Phil.

Relax, you never heard from Hunter again. Maybe it was all nothing but a forgotten deal, my subconscious reminded me.

"How dare you," I said coldly, making sure the tone of my voice would catch him off-guard. My whole body was shaking in anger, and there was nothing else left in my head but to step on his dominance and, for once, give him a nice lesson that he can't just treat me this way ever again.

"What?" he asked, stepping back to confront me again. This time, I took hold of myself, ready to match the level of his ego.

Before I knew it, I hit him.

Did I really slap Commander Blake?

I was stunned for a moment just like him.

Keep your head up, Aiya! Don't look down! My subconscious cheered me on, pushing me to my limits, but it was too late. My tears poured out from my eyes, and I ended up breaking down in front of him.

"I am so tired of you! What have I done to you to be treated this way? Haven't you realized yet? I have risked my life here just like everybody does! I fulfill my duty without even getting paid! I am here to serve the country just like you do! You don't have the right to degrade me! You have no right to regard me as a bitch roaming around and seducing all your soldiers! I almost died out there! We almost died! And Phil?! Phil is still missing!!! Don't you have any decency to at least respect our sacrifices here?"

We glared at each other for a while. I was waiting for him to hit me back, but he didn't. He looked quite bowled over as my tears ran down my cheeks. I was literally crying like a child, and it was the first time I'd seen him speechless.

"What happened here?" Allen's voice suddenly interrupted our unspoken intensity.

Both of us turned to his direction.

"Aiya," he said and reached for me as soon as he saw my tears. He wiped them quickly with his knuckles. "Are you okay?" he asked, trying to catch my stare. Then, he turned to his brother, who was still shocked.

"I'm sorry, this is just too much," I uttered and let go of myself.

Quickly, I ran through the corridor and reached our empty dormitory in no time. I heard Allen calling out my name. He was still chasing me, as if he was the one who had done me wrong. But it wasn't the time to stay calm and let his unthreatening presence console me again.

So, I shut the door and made sure it was locked. I needed time to be alone. I needed my privacy. I was too exhausted and devastated. I wasn't sure if I would be able to forgive Tristan, and it was a pity that the friendship I had with his brother had to suffer, too.

CHAPTER 4

It was still dark when I woke up. What had happened the day before was too much, and I hadn't been able to get up from bed to eat my dinner. I wanted to speak to Riane, but she was already fast asleep by then, and just like me whenever I came back from duty, she needed some sleep.

I prepared myself to report to work lazily. I wanted to quit and leave this camp already, but my conscience would never let me fall asleep again then unless I heard from Phil. I needed to know if he was alright. I needed to know what had happened to him and where he was.

Tears welled in my eyes as I considered how I was caught up in this tormenting situation. Did his safety really depend on me now? What if I'd let Allen know? Maybe, there was something they could do.

I walked the same route I did every day, heading to the camp's clinic. I knew by this time, Allen and his team would be jogging on the nearby lawn. Would it be the perfect time to talk about this?

I took a deep breath as I continued my steps, hoping I would get the chance to speak to him.

But how are you supposed to get near him now? You just shut him down yesterday, my subconscious reminded me.

Yeah, right. Maybe, he is mad at me, too, just like his brother.

So, I dismissed the idea and decided to head straight to the clinic instead. Besides, if Commander Blake saw me again with the soldiers, it would just give him another reason to stand by his false accusation against me, and I didn't think I could handle that.

✶ ✶ ✶

I was feeling really low. I felt guilty for being cold throughout the day. I knew my coworkers noticed my mood and luckily, nobody dared to ask what was wrong. Obviously, no one was aware of the slapping incident yesterday except for Allen. It was quite a relief, but I wondered what was in store for me after I disrespected the commander. Knowing how large his ego was, I was quite sure he wouldn't let it slide easily. To be honest, I was starting to feel uneasy about the things that may happen to me.

"Aiya, would you mind helping me with the inventory?" Riane spoke out, waking me up from my deep reverie. We were at the canteen for lunch, and I had no idea how long I had been staring at my food because it seemed like I hadn't touched it while the others were already packing up.

"Oh, yeah, sure," I said and put down my spoon.

Riane seemed confused when she saw that my plate was still not empty. So, she waited to see if I would continue eating or if I would leave the food uneaten. Since I wasn't starving, I decided to do the second option.

"Are you okay?" she asked, anxiously.

"Yeah, why?" I wondered. Was I that obvious?

"I was expecting you to empty your plate today. Isn't fillet and mushroom soup your favorite meal?" she asked.

"Yes," I agreed. "I'm just not hungry." I moved away the bowl and plate.

Just then, I caught a glimpse of Tristan as he entered the hall. He was glaring at our table, clearly annoyed.

What now? Will he start a fight over my soup?

"Can we go?" I turned to my friend, and she nodded and got on her feet without a protest.

✶ ✶ ✶

Riane was babbling about how she and Sandra had just been talking about their favorite dishes last night at the canteen and had mentioned how much I loved the soup. She clearly wasn't going to let go of my lack of appetite.

"Are you sure you're okay?" she asked again. "You're acting really strange today." She put her arm around my shoulder as if she was expecting me to faint at any moment.

I heaved a deep sigh and stared at her with the saddest expression I could muster. I felt like crying, but the reason behind it was not about Commander Blake at all. I was more concerned about Phil. If I left the camp, it would definitely put him in more danger. The worst part of it was, I couldn't even talk about the matter with anyone.

"Not really," I answered truthfully. She gave me a comforting hug and summoned me to the storage room where we were keeping all the medical supplies.

"What happened?" she asked as soon as we were out of earshot of everybody else.

"I want to quit this mission," I admitted. "I feel like I can't handle the pressure anymore."

"What do you mean? Who's pressuring you?" she asked, completely surprised.

I glanced at her guiltily. I wished I could tell her everything. I shrugged, trying to contain my emotion while she looked at me with her anxious eyes. I knew by the expression on her face, there was no way she would let this conversation be over until she learned the truth. So, I had to come up with another reason. I felt guilty for not telling her the deal I had with Hunter. After all, I still had to make up my mind before doing anything stupid and I hoped, whatever I decided, she would understand.

"Hey," Riane whispered, waking me up again from my deep thoughts. "Why do you want to leave?" she asked, really concerned.

"I slapped the commander's face yesterday," I told her, and her mouth fell opened immediately.

"Y-you… what?!" she exclaimed in disbelief. "But why?"

"I know that was stupid! I was just carried away, Riane," I said as I tried to justify my mistake.

"Oh, jeez! You shouldn't have …" She paused. "So, maybe that's the reason why he looked really upset when he saw you back there."

"You can't blame me! He accused me of seducing all the men in the camp, including the captain," I added, feeling hurt. Why did it suddenly sound like she was on his side?

"Yeah, that's really out of line. But you should have at least considered that he is the commander; he's the boss here," she reminded me, checking the first shelf as she scribbled on her pad.

"Yeah, right. He'll kick me out anyway, but at least I've defended myself before it happens," I said, mirroring her action as I counted the antiseptic in the corner opposite to her. "He can't just mistreat me like that. We're doing a very noble job, and we deserve to be respected. Everybody here deserves that."

Riane put down her list and turned her focus on me. She tapped my shoulder and assured me that she understood. However, like a big sister, she justified the other side of the argument.

"You need to apologize to him," she told me seriously.

"W-what? No way!" I protested vehemently.

"You just said that was stupid. So, you have to take action and make up for your mistake," Riane insisted. "He still is the authority, we should always be respectful."

"It should never be imposed. He needs to earn it," I said, but I knew deep inside of me she was also right. What I did was quite discourteous, and sooner or later, I would need to apologize.

Riane rolled her eyes and by then, I gave in. "Fine, I will, but not now. He owes me an apology as well."

"Really?" she asked in a censuring tone.

"Come on, he is belittling the volunteers. We need some respect, too," I said calmly, trying to be as convincing as possible.

"You're just overthinking things. You're just being too sensitive because you two just didn't have a good start," she said.

"I can't believe you," I uttered, chuckling. "When are you going to take my side?"

"Come on, they did rescue us from the rebels. That alone is enough reason to convince you that they do care for us. We are important to them," Riane continued as if she was a counselor.

"How about Phil? We still haven't heard from him. It looks like they don't even care at all," I said as my heart broke at the thought of him suffering under the hands of the enemies.

"You should understand that it's a confidential matter. We can't just pop up and demand they tell us everything. I'm sure they are doing something to save him. We just have to trust them. It's their job, they know what they're doing."

I didn't respond and continued my task instead. She was right. I was not in a position to question their competence yet, I just felt really impatient at the progress of the mission. It had been half and a month, and still, Phil was nowhere to be seen.

"I know you're worried about Phil. Of course, we all are. But trust me, everything will be alright. All we can do to help is to pray for his safety and for the success of their rescue mission," she continued.

* * *

Everybody in the camp was in good shape. Indeed, it was a hassle-free day for the medical team. No injured or sick personnel needed urgent medical attention. Our senior nurse, Sandra, called it "self-declared holiday" because we were allowed to take the day-off. We were allowed to roam around the site to relax.

"But of course, we can only visit the safe-marked area," she reminded us.

Sandra volunteered to stay at the clinic just in case someone needed any assistance, while Lily and the others chose to have a quick visit to the nearby falls accompanied by some military escorts.

"Do you have other plans in mind?" I asked Riane when she refused to join the group. We were the only two people left in the dormitory.

"I'll take this opportunity to get a whole day nap!" she said dreamily, clutching her thick blanket and throwing herself on the bed.

I chuckled at the thought. "Honestly, you call that a *plan*?" I commented, a little sarcastic.

"Why not? I deserve that," she uttered confidently. "What do you have in mind?"

"I think I'll go and see the greenhouse. Would you like to join me instead?" I wondered, hoping she would change her mind.

Riane turned around, yawning theatrically. "Aiya, you know I'm still your friend. But right now, I'll choose my bed over you, and I hope you'll forgive me," she answered and winked.

✶ ✶ ✶

It was already half past twelve in the afternoon when I reached the greenhouse, which was situated right behind the camp's galley. Luckily, Ramon, the head cook, allowed me to visit.

"The greenhouse is a great help to me, y'know," he said as he led the way. "Especially, yesterday," he added and chuckled. "Commander Tristan suddenly requested fillet mushroom soup menu out of nowhere! It was a good thing we were able to harvest enough mushrooms from here!"

"Really?" I asked, completely intrigued. My subconscious suddenly concluded something, but it felt too good to be true.

Was the meal he requested from Ramon his peace offering to me and he was just too shy to offer it in person? But I immediately disregard the idea. He didn't know anything about my favorite food, and why would he even bother? Unless he'd overheard Riane and Sandra talking the previous night?

Or... maybe it's just a coincidence, I thought.

41

"You know, dear, you're the first and only one from the medical team who actually pays attention to the greenhouse," Ramon continued, grabbing back my attention.

Ramon was very keen to show me every corner of the area, and I must say I really enjoyed it. But after a while, he excused himself and informed me he had to go back to the kitchen.

It was a huge greenhouse, and it was quite amazing how these bunch of plants were able to feed hundreds of soldiers and personnel for years. Although the kitchen staff still needed to get some food supplies from the nearby town, the advantage of harvesting vegetables right at the camp was great.

Aside from that, there was also a small corner for medicinal plants like *neem* and *oregano*. However, these were the only medicinal plants I was familiar with. There were loads of them in different colors and sizes; maybe I would ask Ramon about them one of these days. For now, I just wanted to breathe some fresh air and admire this green and secluded garden.

"Hey," said a familiar voice, and my heart suddenly started beating at a frantic pace. I wasn't ready to face him yet. Turning around, Allen was already behind me.

"H-hey," I said, a little embarrassed.

"How are you?" he asked sincerely.

"Feeling better now, thanks for asking," I answered. "About the other day, I'm really sorry. I was just too upset, I just needed time to be alone."

"Don't worry about it, I understand," Allen responded kindly. "Sorry for my brother's attitude, by the way. I know he's behaving badly lately after the rescue incident."

"I shouldn't have slapped him, I know," I uttered, feeling regretful now. Allen was Tristan's complete opposite, and although I hated his brother, Allen's kind words were making up for it, as if he was gifted with super healing power.

Having a long conversation with Allen without getting bored at all was actually a surprise. I never had an idea that we could stay in this place conversing about anything and everything we could talk about.

"Are you sure I am not keeping you for too long? They must be looking for you," I reminded him as I realized we were together for almost two hours. But before he could even respond, we heard a continuous loud siren echoing around the military compound.

Allen's face became alert, and his hand reached for his gun immediately.

"W-what's that?" I asked him, startled.

"Stay here, I'll take a look," he murmured, summoning me behind the bushes as if our lives were suddenly at stake. He left, and in a few short minutes, he returned.

I stared at him, a little anxious. The scenes of what happened at the rebels' hideout were lurking in my thoughts, but I tried really hard to dismiss the idea. *We're not being attacked again, are we?*

"Someone broke into your dormitory," he told me as if he could read my thoughts.

"What? Who…? I mean…wait! Riane is there! She's alone!" I immediately reported, my heart skipping a little at the thought of my friend's safety.

Allen held my hand firmly and we ran to the medical team's place right away. It was the longest five minutes of my life, fighting the urge to cry as I considered another possible nightmare that was happening. As the siren continued to roll, I could see everyone running in the same direction, opposite to where our quarters were located. At the same time, the soldiers were taking their posts while the others were running to our destination, as well.

As we reached our room, I took a deep breath and stepped in. There were a few military personnel at the door, which made me feel a little uneasy. At the back of my head, I was imagining that at any time, two soldiers would come out of the door carrying a stretcher with Riane's body lying lifeless.

Stop being paranoid, Aiya! My subconscious exclaimed in disapproval.

"Did you catch him?" Allen asked right away to one of his colleagues.

"Negative," Tristan answered behind him, which strangely gave me a chill. Why was it so hard to contain myself whenever I heard his voice?

But at that point, I was reminded of the moment I'd slapped his face. I set aside the ill feeling I had towards him. I was more worried about my friend who was left inside the dormitory.

"Where's Riane?" I asked, and my voice was a little shaky.

There was a pause between our circle before Tristan finally replied. "She's in the meeting room."

"Is she hurt?" Allen inquired, helping me out. Did he notice the awkwardness in my face?

"No," Tristan said, turning to him.

Oh, thank goodness!

"But she seems very traumatized. She wouldn't stop crying hysterically," he continued. "She recognizes the man's face, though."

"Who was it, then?" Allen wondered as I got closer, trying to catch up with what was really going on.

"It was Joe Black, part of the rebel group."

CHAPTER 5

Instead of joining the others heading to the safe hall, I insisted on going and seeing my friend in the meeting room. If she was really traumatized, she didn't deserve this kind of interrogation right now.

Tristan seemed really annoyed at my stubbornness, but he did not argue with me this time, which made me a little taken aback. *Was it really him?* I couldn't believe he'd kept his mouth shut and didn't argue with me for once.

We were quiet, and all we could hear were the sounds of our footsteps in the corridor. I felt relieved knowing that Riane was not physically hurt, but I still had to make sure, so I needed to see her in person.

When we got into the room, I saw my friend sitting on the chair where I'd treated the captain when he cut his hand. She was pale, trembling, and sobbing like a lost and terrified kitten who had been luckily rescued from the jaws of a lion.

"Aiya!" She burst into fresh tears. I rushed to her and gave her a tight embrace, giving her the reassurance that I would not leave her.

"What happened? Are you okay?" I asked, checking her out worriedly. Although her howls subsided, she was still shaking and I had to hold her still and brought her back on her seat.

"I thought he was going to kill me!" she told me, all eyes were on her now.

Allen and some of the soldiers who were listening behind him looked sympathetic except for Commander Tristan who stood in front of us and wasn't on the same wavelength.

"Now, Miss Riane, I need you to tell me what Joe did inside the room," he told her, his voice stern and obviously impatient. It pained me to see and hear that he had absolutely no sympathy for her tears and terror.

How insensitive he is! I silently protested. I glanced at my friend, who seemed to be struggling composing herself, and when she tried to speak up once more, she burst into tears again.

"I already told you, I don't know," she cried. "I was sleeping and when I woke up he's already pointing his gun on my head. He said if I made a noise, he would pull the trigger," she continued, her face horrified as she recalled the incident.

I put my hand on her back and caressed her soothingly.

"What the hell does he want in the medical team's quarter?" Tristan grunted, and his eyes darted to mine before he fixed his attention back on her. But it seemed like he was talking more to himself rather than anyone around. He looked completely frustrated now, but it was a shame that he was trying to put pressure on my traumatized friend.

Riane just shook her head frantically as if she needed to answer the commander. At the same time, she was still in tears. Oh, how this sight was disheartening me! Were they thinking she was with the rebels' side?

"Please, sir, can we give her a break?" I pleaded, trying to control my emotions. I still hated Tristan Blake, but I had to remain calm and respectful, especially at this very moment. "Maybe, we can continue this after she's been checked at the clinic… sir?" I suggested.

Tristan's face turned red, and I knew by then it was a bad idea. Oh, well—when was the last time he'd really listened to someone like me?

"I don't think your opinion matters right now, Miss Shaw," he said, and there was suddenly a complete silence. Even Riane's sobs ceased.

"I disagree, sir," I replied, blood rushing like a blaze of fire ready to consume him. "She's my friend, and my opinion about her welfare matters just like everybody else in this camp."

I didn't shout at him. I didn't even raise my voice. But the cold, firm tone of my delivery was enough for him to recognize my temperament. I'd had enough of him. I'd tried to be courteous. I'd tried to stay calm for a long time.

Riane clutched my wrist swiftly. "I-it's okay, Aiya. Thanks. I-I'll just cooperate," she whispered in a suppressed voice.

Meanwhile, Allen interrupted. He came closer to his brother and murmured, "Maybe it's best if we give them a moment."

Tristan's face turned even more irritated. "Do you hear yourself, Allen? Are you actually taking her nonsense?" he uttered in disgust. Then he turned to me as if I was a pain in his eyes and somehow, it tore my heart apart. How I wished we hadn't started this way. "This woman acts as if she knows everything! And right now? It's not helping! A moment is a waste of our fucking time! Do you get that?!" then he looked around at his men angrily. "DO YOU ALL GET THAT?!"

Everyone was silent, scared at his outburst.

"We still have a hostage to save, and we're still clueless where the hell they took him! Now, if your solution to that fucking problem is to babysit your friend here… then why don't you leave this room right now because you're not even helping! Or better yet, make yourself busy! Go around and flirt with the boys!"

There was a brief moment of tension between us, and I honestly thought everyone was waiting for me to cry or do something childish like breaking down and slapping him again.

"Leave," Tristan ordered me, pointing his finger to the exit.

I held my tears, my face stiff in protest. But I stared him straight in the eyes, keeping my dignity.

I will not cry. I will not give him that satisfaction.

So, I glanced at my friend, making sure she would be okay to be left alone. She nodded at me, quite concerned.

Without a word, I made my way to the exit, sensing all the eyes on me. Allen was the only one who came after me but somehow, I was wishing it was Tristan instead. Why was it so difficult for him to be kind to me?

"I'll be back," I heard Allen said to the team.

As we stepped outside, he tried to console me, but it was unnecessary. I was hurt, of course. But I would be okay. He should attend to more important issues concerning his duties.

"I'm really sorry about that," he said sincerely.

"Please, don't be sorry," I answered kindly. "You don't always have to apologize for your brother's faults."

"Yeah, I know… but… it's just," he mumbled, trying to search for the perfect words to say.

"I'll see you around, Allen. Thanks," I said. "I hope my friend will be a great help to your investigation."

Allen stared at me and smiled sympathetically. "I'll see you around. Would you at least let me escort you to the secure area?"

✷ ✷ ✷

It took us a few more hours before finally, everyone was released. I wondered where Riane was, hoped she was fine. Sandra was worried about her, too, but for our safety, she ordered all the medical teams to stay indoors and call it a day. After all, it was already late in the evening, and we would be reporting for duty in the morning as usual.

"I wonder what that criminal has to do with our dormitory, particularly in your unit?" she wondered as we head our way back.

"Yeah, it makes me wonder, too," Lily said.

"Is it because the three of you stay there together?" Sandra inquired, anxious.

"What do you mean?" I asked, but the hint was actually making sense now.

"I'm just thinking that you, Lily and Riane are roommates. And your group was successfully rescued by the government. Maybe, it has something to do with your captivity before?" Sandra concluded, and my heart suddenly skipped a beat.

"What would they want from us?" Lily said, her tone still confused.

"I don't know. Maybe, they wanted to take you hostage again or something," Sandra answered, and her face went pale and worried. "Oh my god, I hope it's not. I'm just being paranoid. Maybe, it's just a coincidence."

51

We bid farewell to our head nurse as we stepped through the door. Although the camp was now declared safe, there were still soldiers roaming around the area, especially outside our unit.

"It's been a long day, huh?" Lily uttered as soon as she slumped on her bed.

"Yeah," I said and sighed, recalling what happened. From the wonderful time spent in the greenhouse to the awful words I heard from Commander Tristan Blake, and to the possible motives of Joe Black.

"Will Riane be alright? Have you seen her?" she asked one last time before turning off her bedside lamp.

"Yeah, I think she will be fine," I answered. I really had no idea where was she, but thinking that she'd be accompanied by Allen's team was enough to settle down my worries.

I lay on my bed and waited until finally, I heard Lily snoring. My thoughts were not letting me sleep at all. I could sense that Joe Black's breaking in was not a mere coincidence.

He is after me.

I shivered at the thought. This was the moment I had been dreading. Hunter probably sent him to remind me of our deal, and it was torturing my whole being right now. So, I got up and looked around, nothing seemed really strange in the room, but there had to be something. He must have done something here before Riane saw him.

The first thing that caught my attention was the position of my hairbrush on the bedside table. I was sure I'd put it in my drawer before leaving for work this morning. How come it was now on top?

I took a deep breath; the tension was consuming me. I felt a cold sweat suddenly invade my face as I struggled to get on my feet to find out what was waiting for me. The drawer was half-opened and I was pretty sure someone ransacked my stuff and only I would notice. I was very particular about every detail of my personal belongings, and this drawer being left half-opened wasn't something I would do.

I looked around first as if worried that I would get caught by someone. Then, I scurried and kneeled on the floor to reach my personal drawer, scared to find out if my intuition was correct.

And there… right there on top of my diary where my hairbrush used to sit lay a pink brand of feminine wash I hadn't ever tried.

I knew by then something was wrong about it. The liquid was supposed to be pink in color and not crystal clear.

This is not happening…

CHAPTER 6

I didn't sleep for the whole night. I lay awake, waiting for the dawn to come. Nurses are actually used to the graveyard shift, but the effect of not catching up on my sleep last night was different. Added to this was the overwhelming anxiety that I was feeling. Reality hit me like a punch in the gut—*Phil is still alive and his life really depends on me now. What should I do?*

Secretly, I pulled the small bottle from underneath my pillow where I'd hidden it and put it in the bag where I kept my toiletries, which were all handy. No one would suspect it was something for sure.

Thank goodness, Riane was back. She and Lily were peacefully asleep on their beds. Anyway, it was my shift today, so it was not a big deal for them to get extra hours of rest. Hastily, I dragged myself to the bathroom and brought the pouch with me. Before I got myself ready, I decided to take a quick test of the liquid in the strange bottle.

Pulling out a leaf from the indoor plant placed on the side of the sink, I put a small droplet of the substance. In a few seconds, the leaf melted in front of my eyes.

"Oh," I gasped in horror. "What kind of…?" I was stunned, trembling. In a moment, I was suddenly in a panic, pacing back and forth across the bathroom.

"Shit," I uttered nervously. "I can't do this to them!"

I was not really sure how long I sat on the floor before finally, I took a shower and composed myself again.

I'm in big trouble! my mind kept telling me as I headed to the clinic.

Distracted, I didn't notice Tristan until we were face to face. He literally snapped his fingers to wake me up from my deep reverie.

"Do you mind?" he said, irked by my absentmindedness.

I was stunned to see him standing in front of me, waiting for me to give way since the path was too narrow to accommodate us both at a time.

"Oh," I said, disoriented. I moved aside and waited for him to walk by. I had no time to argue at that moment.

"No, you first," he said, his tone irritated as usual.

So, without a word, I obliged. My silence probably confused him.

"Are you okay?" he called out, and when I turned back to him, his expression looked so concerned.

I stared at him, mouth open, unable to respond. *Did he really just ask me that?*

After an awkward moment, Tristan shook his head and cleared his throat. "Never mind," he said. "Miss Shaw, you should eat regularly to keep your mind alert," he added bitterly, obviously referring to the fillet and mushroom soup that I hadn't touched.

I stood there and watched him leave. That was the first time he'd asked me if I was okay with a sincere look on his face. I loved that the worried look was meant for me. I could almost feel his desire to take my anxiety away.

I suddenly wanted to throw myself in his arms and let out a good cry, tell him how scared I was and how I needed his comfort. But it was impossible. All I could do was stare at him as he continued to walk away, leaving me shaken and unheard.

✳ ✳ ✳

"Having a deep thought?" Allen's voice woke me up from my contemplation. It took a while before I remembered where I was.

"H-hey," I greeted him, trying to put on a smile on my face. "What are you doing here?"

"Well, I saw you came in early, and you look so low. I think you need this to cheer you up or simply to warm your stomach," he said, handing me a cup of hot coffee.

"Oh, thanks," I answered appreciatively. "How kind of you."

"Any time," he said and occupied the seat opposite my desk. "How are you?" I raised an eyebrow immediately, so he raised his hands promptly to defend himself. "I'm not talking about Tristan, okay? I mean, it is just a casual how are you question from a friend who's catching up."

"Okay." I chuckled. "I'm fine," I lied, trying to sound as normal as possible. Should I tell him about the poison? About the real reason why Joe Black broke in into camp?

Don't even think about it. They may accuse you even more and put you in jail, my subconscious called in a rush.

"How's the investigation about last night going?" I asked him, hoping he would sprinkle even just a little bit of information, although I knew Riane would disclose everything to me later.

Meanwhile, Allen seemed to be enjoying my initiative, but it didn't seem like he would give away the details.

"To be honest, I was surprised Riane cooperated with us so well after the confrontation you had with Tristan," he answered.

"And?" I asked again, urging him to tell me more.

Allen sighed, then he shook his head apologetically. "I'm sorry, I can't tell you."

I nodded. "Squealing is punishable, huh? Don't worry about it, I don't want to lose a friend like you, so I won't force you," I said and smiled. Then, I took the time to finish my cup. It was a great coffee indeed.

✶ ✶ ✶

Riane seemed to be coping much better already. She had started forgetting the trauma she had from the night Joe Black burst in and pointed his weapon towards her. In fact, she always joined me and Allen during lunchtime and dinner. Sometimes, we'd do a quick walk around at the greenhouse, as well, to make her feel better.

"Can I ask you something?" my friend asked.

It was Lily's duty at the clinic, so we were left alone in the dormitory together.

"Sure, what is it?" I asked casually while sitting on my bedside and folding my newly laundered clothes.

"It's obvious that Lieutenant Allen is into you. So, I wondered, do you like him too? Or are you falling in love with him already?" she asked, curious and attentively waiting for me to respond.

"What made you ask all of a sudden?" I said, blushing at her query. It was something I wasn't ready to talk about.

"Well? Would you answer my question first, before I answer yours?" she said, raising her eyebrow theatrically.

To be honest, I took my time to actually assess my feelings for Allen. Sure thing, he was quite a catch. I mean, he was handsome, a gentleman, thoughtful and caring. In fact, I could tell the girls in the camp, including my best friend, were all attracted to him because of his charming personality. He was brave and skilled, and he had a heart for his men, unlike his brother, who had nothing else in mind but his ego. But I couldn't help but think of his brother instead.

Tristan.

"I would be a hypocrite if I said I hadn't noticed?" I replied sincerely.

"So, tell me, are the two of you together? Like a boyfriend and girlfriend kind of romance?" Riane prodded, giggling.

"Of course not!" I said immediately.

"Not yet?" she interrogated.

"It's not like I have a plan, dear," I assured her. "I want to focus here. Besides, the commander will suspect again that I'm trying to seduce his brother."

"So, what? It's not like you're going to have to be his girlfriend, too!" she said and rolled her eyes.

I wish…

"You don't understand. Tristan has his full attention on me. I think he is picking on me in particular, and I'm confused about why he hates me that much," I told her, feeling a little critical now.

"Maybe he's jealous," Riane answered, shrugging her shoulders with pouted lips.

I laughed at the thought, but suddenly, my heart was hoping. "That's ridiculous," I exclaimed and threw a pillow at her.

"Come on, it's possible! Besides, men have different ways of expressing their emotions. It so happens that Commander Tristan is poor at it."

✶ ✶ ✶

It had been two weeks since the incident with Joe Black. Since then, it had become quiet again, but I wasn't so sure if I should feel happy about it or not. Were they just waiting for our deal to materialize?

Riane and Lily were not able to join me for lunch, so instead of heading straight to the dining hall, I decided to stay in the clinic and do the inventory. I must admit I was restless since the break-in, and for once in my life, I feared for my life, for Phil's and for everyone who might get involved with this coming catastrophe. The problem was that I felt like it all depended on my decision. Whether I'd do it or not, someone would still suffer the consequences.

"Hey, Aiya," Allen greeted. "Is everything okay?"

"Yeah," I said, putting up a front again. I had no idea how many times I had lied to him already.

"Are you sure? You don't look like you're okay," he commented, trying to look into my eyes.

"I'm just feeling a little low these days, you know," I answered, trying to avoid eye contact. It's not that I was self-conscious because of his stare, I was just scared he would see that I was hiding something from him. Somehow, I had this gut feeling that Allen was treating me extra special because he was spying on me or something.

That's some sort of guilt anxiety, my mind snapped shortly when the thought suddenly hit my head.

"Sorry to hear that," Allen said, a little disappointed.

"Why do you always apologize?" I asked, letting out a soft chuckle.

Allen grinned, scratching his head. It was cute in a boyish way. No wonder the girls were so mesmerized by his bewitching charm. But all I could think about was what cute little habits his brother might have.

"I don't know, it always comes out naturally," he answered in humor.

"Anyway, Aiya, I'd like to ask you something," he said after a while.

"Sure, what is it?" I wondered, putting down my pen and paper.

"Are you free tonight? Can we spend some time in the greenhouse together? There's something I want to show you," he said, hopeful.

"Oh, no problem. I'm sure Riane would love to visit the place again, too!" I told him enthusiastically.

But Allen looked embarrassed. "I mean, just the two of us this time," he clarified immediately.

Oh! So, he wanted to spend some time alone with me. Was he going to admit his feelings for me already?

No, you have no time for romance, Aiyana, my mind reminded me right away.

I glanced at him. Allen was a beautiful and kind creature; it would be a torture to decline his invitation. He'd always been nice to me. He was one of the reasons why I was still around at this moment. But the first thing that crossed my mind was Tristan's reaction to this.

Why am I so worried about his opinion?

"So, what do you think? Is it too much to ask right now?" he asked, and I didn't understand why I suddenly felt guilty about his response.

"Of course not," I told him, trying to cheer up the mood. "I would like to go."

His charming smile came back.

"Really, that's great! It's the best birthday gift I received today so far," he said happily.

"Oh, it's your birthday today?" I asked, a little caught off-guard.

"Yeah."

"Oh! I'm so sorry! I had no idea! Happy birthday!" I gave him a quick, friendly hug.

"Thanks, no worries," he answered, blushing a little. "So, I guess, I will see you later?"

"Yeah, sure."

✶ ✶ ✶

I had no time to change into my casual clothes, so I went straight to the greenhouse wearing my uniform. I was feeling uneasy, and I had no idea why. I guess I was starting to overthink things since that incident. Or perhaps, I was worried about giving Allen false hope.

Why would Allen want us to be alone? The thought made me shiver. I could tell he liked me, but I wasn't ready to return the same feelings. In fact, I was still confused about how I felt for his brother. Sure, Tristan was rude to me. But I couldn't help it. It was he who always crossed my mind.

Allen was already sitting on the bench near the medicinal plant section. He smiled sincerely as soon as he saw me approaching him.

"Hi," I greeted him and smiled back. "What do you have in there?" I asked him when I saw a brown paper bag beside him.

He stood up and welcomed me like a true gentleman. "Just some snacks," he answered casually.

"Oh, that's nice," I replied. It would be great if I had been notified of his birthday a few days early. "I'm sorry, I should have gotten you something," I said.

"Oh, please don't bother," he replied. "Having you here with me tonight is already enough for me."

Damn, this was weird.

"Are you hungry?" he asked, defying the awkward silence between us.

"I skipped my lunch, so yeah, I'm hungry now," I answered, chuckling.

So, we sat down on the bench, ate the sandwiches and drank from the bottle of water he brought. It was nice to spend some time with someone who would simply sit beside you and demand nothing but a moment of quiet.

"You know, sometimes I think, what if I didn't sign up for this job?" Allen said, his voice turning wistful.

I turned to him and tried to read between the lines. "Are you regretting your chosen profession?" I asked him.

"No, not all," he answered, defensive. "But have you ever experienced at some point in your life that you're too fed up with an everyday routine?"

Yeah, I have.

"Are you tired of the military?" I asked him instead.

Allen's face became sad. "I'm tired of this war," he answered sincerely.

Oh, I didn't see that coming.

He continued speaking out his sentiments. "This is a beautiful world, Aiya. But nobody noticed the flowers or even the trees and plants around this place. Why? Because everyone is too busy killing each other."

This was the only time Allen had revealed another side of himself. Since when had he been so emotional about such things?

"You're right," I agreed with him.

"It's funny, you know. When I was younger, I dreamed of studying botany. Who would ever think I would end up in the military?" he said and laughed, but I could sense it was a forced one.

"That's not a surprise at all," I commented, and it actually surprised him.

"Really? Why do you say so?" he wondered, and there was a bright hope evident in his eyes as if he was pleased to hear what I had observed about him.

"Well, when you gave me the stem of middlemist, I could tell you have an eye for plants and flowers," I answered truthfully, and he smiled even more at the notion.

"Wow, I can't believe you were so perceptive," he said, his expression in complete awe.

"Come on," I answered and laughed. "Thanks for inviting me, by the way. You really know when I need to get a breath of fresh air. It is such a unique way to celebrate someone's birthday," I continued and grinned at him kindly.

Allen smiled back, his face was guilty. "Actually…" he murmured, completely flushed. "It's not really my birthday," he admitted.

"What?" I smirked, playfully raising my eyebrow.

"I just made it up," he confessed. "I was worried you wouldn't accept my invitation without Riane's company, so I had to find a way to make you say yes."

I chuckled, feeling really weird. I know I should feel offended. But I couldn't find any trace of ill emotion towards him. Perhaps, it was because he had been good to me since we met and of course, I owed my life to him. He saved me and my team from the enemy.

"Why would you do that?" I asked him in a light and amused tone of voice.

"Well… I just want to spend some time with you alone," he admitted, and I wished there was something I could do to postpone the moment. I didn't want to break his heart. He was such a good friend, and with all the stress in my life at present, I didn't want to lose any friends.

"Aiya," Allen whispered, and suddenly he became serious. "I'm in love with you, and I can't hide this anymore. From the short time that we have spent together, I knew you're the only girl that I want to share my life with."

I was stunned to hear the gravity of Allen's desire.

The only girl he wants to share his life with?

That was too much to process. I was only expecting him to say that he liked me. There was a brief silence between us, and I could sense that he was trying to figure out an answer through my facial reaction. The tension was too high; I could almost pass out.

"No pressure," he assured me, and it was then I found myself breathing again. "I just want to take advantage of the moment to tell you how I feel."

I liked him as a friend. I couldn't get into a relationship right now, let alone with someone I didn't even think I had feelings for. I already had too much to handle, and this was not the right time for romance. And what if we ended up getting married? How could I survive having Tristan as my brother-in-law?

"You're a good man, Allen," I said. "But I hope you won't misunderstand. I just feel like I'm not ready yet," I continued, and he nodded responsively like a brave and true gentleman. "I'll be honest, I have a lot on my mind right now. And I'm looking forward to leaving this mission without extra baggage."

"I understand," he said. "You don't need to love me back. But at least, let me show you how sincere I am. Who knows? Sooner or later, you might be ready to accept me?"

Was this really happening? I hadn't met a man as selfless and as determined as him.

Allen stared at me tenderly, and before I knew it, I felt his lips touching mine.

Before I had a chance to process what was happening, we heard a voice and jerked apart, startled.

"Allen!!"

Shit! It's Tristan!

He was standing at the greenhouse's entrance, glaring angrily at us. It was the most frightening expression I had seen in his face, and I knew I was in big trouble. *We* were actually in trouble. But since Tristan and Allen were brothers, I was hoping he wouldn't find himself in too much trouble.

"Tristan, what are you doing here?" he asked abruptly, shielding me as if his brother would attack me or something.

"What are you doing here? With her?" he asked and darted at me. I looked away, embarrassed and humiliated.

"Give her a break, bro," Allen pleaded, but Tristan stepped closer, his eyes fixed on mine. He was angry, but his eyes were… *jealous?*

"Now, tell me you weren't bitching around my men, Miss Shaw," he hissed at me, his tone threatening and disgruntled. *Guess he's not jealous.*

Allen pulled him away. Then he held my face dearly. "I'm sorry about this. I'll talk to you soon, okay?" he whispered and kissed my forehead before leaving.

"Stop this nonsense, Allen! We need you at the meeting room, NOW!" Tristan ordered angrily, not leaving his brother behind.

In no time, they marched away, and I was left alone watching their silhouettes fade away through the darkness.

I waited for a few more minutes to calm myself. I wanted to cry. I wanted to burst into tears. I wanted to run to Commander Tristan and explain my side. I wanted to prove to him that I was no slut.

CHAPTER 7

The next morning, I realized I overslept. So, I hurried to get myself ready and zoomed my way to the clinic so I could report for duty on time.

Meanwhile, as I was on my way through the corridor, the female soldiers were giving odd glances, and as much as I wanted to ask them what the problem was, I couldn't compromise my log-in time, especially now that the commander's full attention was completely on me.

"Aiyana, can I talk to you for a minute?" Sandra called as soon as she saw me.

"S-sure," I said and followed her to the office. I was worried she would scold me for coming late today, but I realized quickly that it was more serious than I had in mind.

Sandra's expression was stern. Her usual cheerful mood was missing, and I knew I was in bigger trouble. I could sense it had something to do with what happened last night, but to what extent? How serious would that particular incident be?

"What's wrong?" I asked her politely.

Sandra shook her head. She was obviously struggling for words. Then, she patted my hand softly as if already consoling my confounded mind.

"This is nothing personal, Aiyana," she started. "But Commander Blake issued an order against you. He is canceling your permit as our volunteer staff in the camp. He is sending you back to the city hospital."

I stared at her blankly, trying to contain the whole weight of the situation.

"B-but why? What have I done?" I asked but I already knew the answer.

Sandra held out a signed memo and handed it to me. I took my time to read it, and my whole body was shaking in anger. Commander Blake was accusing me of moral misconduct, citing the kissing incident he personally witnessed.

"He is really not going to stop," I uttered, my voice was trembling in fury.

"Aiya, I have nothing against you. You're smart and competent. Whatever you and the Lieutenant have, it's none of my business at all. It's your personal affair. But there is nothing I can do about this," she said, regretfully.

"It's not true," I defended. "I never provoked nor seduced anybody."

"I know, I believe you," she said and gave me a comforting hug. "I'm so sorry."

"I-I can't leave right now," I appealed to her. I needed this for my internship requirement, but I was more concerned with Phil's welfare. If I left, things might get even worse.

Sandra was obviously suppressing her tears. Finally, we let go of each other.

"When will be my last day?" I asked her after a while. I needed to speak with that douche. I hadn't seen Allen around, so I bet he sanctioned him, too.

"Tomorrow," she answered sadly. "You'll be escorted to the town and taken to the train station."

✳ ✳ ✳

Everything made sense now. So, this was the reason why I was getting foul stares from everyone. I wondered if Lily and Riane were aware of the issue already.

I left my post immediately and rushed to Commander Blake's office. But he was not there. I hated him! I hated him so much it was very hard to contain the emotion.

Where the hell was he?!

I roamed around, searching for his whereabouts until finally, I found him leading Allen's platoon.

Had he suspended his brother, too?

I headed straight to the field, climbing over the barricades to reach their area. I knew he was already aware of my presence, but still, I waited a few meters away from him, hoping he would excuse himself from the group for a talk. But the sun was getting hotter above me, and if I stayed much longer, I would pass out.

So, I marched to the platoon and faced him directly, ignoring the confused group of soldiers under his command.

"Commander Blake, may I have a word with you?" I asked firmly.

He paused, and his eyes darted directly to me. It was a mocking glare I would never forget.

"So, looks like you already received your memo?" he asked, sarcastic, and it was breaking my heart how it was so easy for him to hurt me just by that stare. "Pack your things early, Miss Shaw. You'll be leaving before the break of dawn."

71

"I don't accept this!" I exclaimed angrily. "Just because your brother likes me doesn't mean I am a foul fucking bitch!"

There was an awkward silence. I knew all eyes were on me now, but I didn't give a damn. I had been trying to be as respectful as possible, but kicking me out of the volunteer program was too much to bear.

He was stunned, but he kept his composure. Then, he finally excused himself and allowed one of his men to take over the routine.

"Follow me," he ordered and headed to his office.

I had a hard time keeping up, but I managed to do it anyway, wondering what was really going on his mind. As soon as he let me in, he shut and locked the door without uttering a word.

Then, he leaned on his desk and stared at me, waiting. I took a deep breath, maintaining the fierceness I mustered in full effort.

"What now?" he mumbled, provoking.

"This is too much. What's wrong with you?" I asked, angrily. I could feel my blood boiling, rushing through my face.

"Shouldn't I be the one asking that?" His face was malicious.

"You can't do this to me right now," I insisted, feeling frustrated. What else could I do, anyway?

"Yes, I can, Miss Shaw," he said arrogantly. "Would that be all or you're going to barter something with me to cancel my order?" he continued, maliciously checking me out from head to toe.

I'd had too much of the insult. For the second time, I slapped his face, tears streaming from my eyes.

"How dare you! How dare you!" I cried, my whole body shaking in anger as I put all my effort into hurting him physically. That was the best thing I could do to avenge the pain he was causing me.

"What the fuck?" he growled as I accidentally scratched his face.

"Where's Allen?! What did you to him?!" I yelled, thinking that he punished him more.

Suddenly, the satisfaction he had in his face morphed into anger. In a snap, he pinned me to the wall, his eyes on fire.

"Don't you dare ask about my brother again," he threatened.

Then suddenly, he claimed my mouth with his. It was not a sweet and tender kiss. Tristan's kisses were torturous. It was angry and punishing.

"Let me go!" I yelled, trying to push him away, but he was too strong to resist.

 It was tormenting and degrading. I tried to kick him with all my strength, but he was quite powerful.

His mouth was feasting, sucking my lips and neck.

Oh, no, he is really going to take me right now. What have I done?

"Please, please stop!" I begged him, but it was like he had been possessed or something. His face was dark and angry... and again, I wondered, *jealous?*

He bit my lower lip forcefully, and I cried in protest at the pain.

Suddenly, he stopped. His dark, smoldering expression had vanished. He stared at me, my face full of tears and my lower lip bleeding. I was sobbing hysterically. This was the first time I'd broken down in front of anybody.

I slumped on the floor, feeling hurt and exhausted while Tristan stood in front of me, completely petrified as if he had been awakened from a deep sleep. He looked guilty and confused.

"Why are you doing this to me?" I whispered, sobbing.

He didn't answer, but fortunately, he came to his senses. Instead, he silently walked away and left me all alone in the room, completely traumatized.

❧ CHAPTER 8 ❧

I was waving goodbye to Riane from a distance until finally, she was out of view. Still, I couldn't believe I was actually leaving the military base this early.

I settled down, remained quiet in the back seat of the four-by-four vehicle while Commander Tristan Blake was in the passenger's seat, speaking with the driver who was also armed and in uniform.

After giving instructions to our two companions, he remained quiet as if he was not aware of my presence.

Oh, the evil is giving you a break, my subconscious teased, enjoying the serenity of the moment.

The other soldier who was right beside me tried to break the ice by initiating a conversation, but I was not in the mood for chit-chat. I was thinking of a better way to save Phil while I was still in the area. But how would I even find him? Indeed, the only answer to my problem was the deadly poison I was carrying inside the purse in my hand.

But I couldn't bear killing and taking innocent lives, and I couldn't bear to see Phil's lifeless body, either. My mother used to tell me that I should always consider the welfare of the majority, but this time, I didn't think it was really applicable.

Phil was very close to me, and he also had a family waiting for him just like everybody at the base.

I clutched my purse tighter and looked away, memorizing each path we were crossing just in case I had to go back and trace my way back into the mountain. I knew it was a stupid idea to search for the enemies, sneak around and rescue Phil on my own. That way, I didn't need to choose between my loyalty to my friend and loyalty to my countrymen.

Are you being serious right now? My mind protested. *You can't even protect yourself from Blake.*

After a three-hour journey, we finally arrived at the mainland. Life here was different but somehow alive. We headed straight to the town, where the central terminal was located. The memory of the medical team's arrival was still vivid in my head as if I could see them standing at the platform, waiting for the military escorts.

I couldn't help but felt a little sentimental. Phil had been the happiest that day. He was so excited to work with the military, but it was not happening now. All that was left to do was hope and pray that he was still as cheerful and carefree as he normally was. Moreover, I was begging the heavens to protect him until help came.

"I'm sorry, Commander, but the train left twenty minutes ago," I heard from the employee who was trying to calm Tristan down, but I wasn't so sure if he was succeeding. His two escorts were just glancing at each other, probably mentally discussing the upcoming mood swings again.

I shuddered as soon as they spotted me in the corner, observing the three of them back and forth.

"When is the next scheduled trip?" he asked impatiently.

The employee spluttered, "It would be the day after tomorrow, sir."

"Damn it!" Tristan said, completely annoyed, but there was nothing he could do about it.

It was probably a good sign after all. Maybe, it was not yet my time to leave.

After a while, Tristan came back to us, looking even more frustrated. He didn't need to explain what happened because obviously, he knew we already heard the conversation he had with the ticket booth employee.

"So, are we going back to the camp?" I asked him after a while.

"No, there's no reason for you to stay there. Besides, it will be dark soon. It's not safe for us to travel back tonight," he informed us.

Commander Blake said it would be best if we waited for the next trip to the town instead of heading back to the camp and probably missing the train again. He was really determined to send me back to the city, and it was painful to think how it was so easy for him not to care.

So, we roamed around and found a travel inn near the train station. Then, without any second thought, he booked two rooms for our group. One for me, and one for him and his men.

"This is not the plan," I uttered when the old woman at the front desk was finally out of earshot and our two escorts were left to buy our dinner.

Tristan looked at me and raised an eyebrow. "Well, do you have other alternatives aside from driving back?" he said, sounding sarcastic.

"I'm just saying you guys don't need to stay in town for days. You can go back tomorrow to the field and I'll just wait for the train myself," I suggested, thinking I would just ruin whatever their schedule was for the next few days.

"Not a chance, Miss Shaw," he answered and smirked. "I have to make sure you really board the train."

"W-what?" I mumbled, feeling a little offended. "I won't run away! In fact, I'd love to leave this place as soon as possible," I lied, trying to make myself feel better. I wanted to give him the impression that his kick-out letter was actually to my advantage.

"Really? Well, I'm sorry, but I don't trust girls like you," he answered, and it was infuriating my female ego once again. Why *did* he hate me so much?

Rolling my eyes, I walked away from him and sat on the old couch in the lobby area. He mirrored my action with a smile on his face and sat opposite my seat. We waited silently until the front desk informed us that the rooms were ready to accommodate us.

Tristan got two sets of keys. He left the other one to the lady and instructed her to give it to our escorts once they returned. He had an audible small talk with the old lady before he approached me and gave me a sweet, lovely smile.

"Come on, honey," he said, theatrically. "Our room is ready."

What the hell? Our room? Honey? I threw him a questioning look.

I stood up, sensing the adoration of the old lady towards us until we climbed to the stairs.

"What the hell was that?" I interrogated him on our way. He just chuckled but didn't answer back.

Finally, we reached a door bearing the number 211. He unlocked it and allowed me to step in. To my surprise, he joined me inside and went straight to lie down on the mattress.

"Are you being serious?" I asked him.

"What?" he asked, a wild grin on his face as he watched me in panic.

"We're not sharing this room, are we?" I asked, completely anxious now. I could still remember what he did to me yesterday.

Tristan got up. This time, he sat on the side of the bed and stared at me with a warning look.

"As I told you, I don't trust someone like you, Miss Shaw. So, obviously, I am here to keep an eye on you. Nothing more, nothing less," he said.

"Why would I even run away and get lost in this place anyway? What makes you think I'll do that? I'd rather go back home and live in the city comfortably," I said, trying to justify myself.

He shrugged and stood up, circling me slowly. "I don't know. I just have this gut feeling that you are up to no good," he said. "Are you, Miss Shaw?" he whispered in my ear, and I shuddered at the gesture, heat pooling in my belly.

I shivered discreetly for a second as his breath touched my earlobes. But I remained still, fighting hard not to blush and stutter. He was so close to me that if I turned to look at him right now, our lips would be touching.

"You're unbelievable," I spat and walked away, heading straight to the bathroom nervously, my purse still in my hand, and the butterflies in my stomach started rumbling inside of me.

I locked the door, then stared at my face in the mirror hanging on the wooden wall. Damn, I was literally blushing. Carefully, I put down my purse on the sink.

"What's happening to you?" I whispered, talking to my reflection. "Do you like that freaking guy?"

I heaved a deep sigh, still staring at myself. Tristan's words suddenly occupied my head, and suddenly, the illusion faded away.

"I don't know. I just have this gut feeling that you are up to no good. Are you, Miss Shaw?"

Did he know something? Did he suspect me as a spy? A part of the rebel group?

I pulled out the small bottle containing the harmful substance which Joe Black left in my drawer. I studied it for a minute or so, still feeling bewildered.

Phil, I thought sadly. *What am I going to do?*

All of a sudden, Tristan was knocking on the bathroom door loudly. "How long are you going to stay there? Our dinner is served!" he informed me, his voice still as impatient as ever.

So, I hurried, putting back the bottle. I washed my face quickly and dried myself with one of the clean towels folded on top of the shelf beside me.

When I got out, the meal was ready. I suspected he'd ordered it from room service, or it was his men who'd brought it? But I wasn't hungry. I had lost my appetite because of his presence.

"I'm not hungry," I told him.

"Really? You're not hungry? We haven't eaten anything since we left the camp," he pointed out.

All of a sudden, there was a knock on the door. I was about to answer it, but Tristan stopped me. Instead, he answered it himself.

"Morgan," he acknowledged and nodded. It was one of the

military escorts who accompanied us here.

"Sir," Morgan replied and handed him something before he left again.

When Tristan came back to view, he was carrying my luggage. He put it on the bed and returned to the small dining table where our dinner was served.

"I asked him to get it for you. You surely need it," he said without looking.

I refrained from saying, 'thanks.' Luckily, I succeeded. But anyway, it didn't look like he was actually expecting me to be grateful for his act. Besides, it wasn't really him who'd delivered my trunk, so he actually didn't deserve the recognition. Morgan did.

"You should stop dieting," he uttered after a while as he helped himself to the food he ordered. "Girls look better with curves," he added, smirking.

"I don't care about your opinion," I told him. "Besides, I'm not trying to lose weight, I just lost my appetite."

Without being obvious, I slid my purse out of view. At the same time, I carefully searched through my stuff and found a comfortable jogger and shirt to wear for the night. I had no plans of wearing my usual sleepwear since it might provoke him again or give him the idea that once again, I was whoring around.

I pretended to be asleep the whole evening. I was too anxious and worried. Anxious about what would be in store for me, and worried that Tristan would come to my bed and force me to sleep with him.

However, none of my worries materialized. Commander Blake did not even lay his back on the bed. Instead, he stayed on the veranda, sitting on watch. I wondered how he patiently managed to remain still until the dawn broke and the sunrise swiftly washed away the dark clouds in the sky.

There were moments I tried to get a glimpse of him. He may have been on watch, but it seemed like he was in deep thought. The reflection of his face through the dim glow of the moon last night was still vivid. What was bothering him?

I remembered the time when Allen justified his brother's behavior to me. I thought somehow I understood what he meant now. Commander Tristan Blake was under stress and pressure. The weight of his responsibilities in the military was obviously consuming him. I couldn't believe I was feeling a little sympathetic all of a sudden.

Before the sun completely set, he went out of the room. Maybe, he was into a morning walk or something. Anyway, good for him. I'd thought he was going to stay there the whole time like a statue.

Eventually, I decided to leave the bed, taking advantage of my sole moment to have a quick shower and fix myself. To be honest, it was just too awkward bathing with a man in the room.

Tristan was still nowhere to be seen when I returned. I bet he was being considerate in giving me much-needed privacy.

But... I thought he was keeping an eye on you? my mind interrupted.

Perhaps, I finally convinced him that I wouldn't run away.

So, I waited, but a few more hours passed and still, he was not around.

But then again, I reminded myself that I'd be more comfortable without him nearby. I was not hungry at all, but since there was orange juice and a sandwich neatly placed on the dining table, I helped myself and ate my breakfast, giving my stomach something to work on throughout the day.

However, there was nothing else left to do inside, and I was starting to get bored.

Maybe, I'll have a quick stroll outside, I thought.

So, I decided to fix my hair and headed to the door, excitedly grabbing the knob. To my dismay, I realized it was locked.

Damn, he locked me in! He was not really letting me out.

I tried unlocking the door several times, hoping I was just wrong. I was trying to convince myself that maybe it was just hard for the knob to work properly because it was a bit rusty. Maybe there was a manual technique or something to hit the unlock.

But then, I found myself giving up. Completely tired and annoyed, I went back to the bed and turned on the television instead to entertain myself.

Out of boredom, I dozed off to sleep again.

"Aiya! Please, save me!" Phil's voice echoed around the dark tunnel but I was having a hard time finding him.

"PHIL!" I called out.

"Please, Aiya!" he yelled in pain. "Ahhh… no!" he cried as if he was begging for someone's mercy.

Was somebody torturing him? I panted, trying to run back and forth amidst the dark surrounding.

"Phil! Tell me where you are!" I shouted, almost breathless. I was tired and sweating terribly. I had been running around the forest for days, searching for him.

"I'm here! I'm just here!" Phil's voice occupied my head.

I followed the echoes, stumbling and getting up again from time to time. And there! There was a light, and I saw Phil's silhouette from afar. He was tied to a large tree, his eyes blindfolded.

"Phil..." I whispered. "I'm coming... I'll save you..."

I rushed towards him, but just before I could reach him, Hunter blocked the view. His eyes were glinting with disappointment, and his sharp, menacing grin wrapped me in fear.

"This is not how we discussed it, Miss Aiyana Shaw," he said, reaching my face. "This is not how Phil shall be saved."

"Please, I don't want to do this anymore. Please, let us go."

His cold hand cupped my chin tightly. "I'm giving you another chance to do it. You know, I am not fond of people who back out of a contract. Remember our deal."

Hunter signaled to his men, who suddenly appeared in the view. One of them, Joe Black, dragged my exhausted friend away from the woods. Phil seemed lifeless now. He was not moving.

"PHIL!" I desperately called out.

"Don't worry, we just put him to sleep," Hunter said, mockingly.

Soon enough they were gone, and I was left alone in the dark and silent heart of the Sylvania Mountain.

"NO!!!!"

I forced myself to wake up. I knew it was just a dream. A nightmare that seemed too real as if I had my third eye opened temporarily, allowing me to take a peek at what Phil was going through right now.

I cried hysterically. A loud, howling cry. I felt the weight of guilt. If they killed Phil, I would not be able to forgive myself. I had to do something, but complying with the deal I had with Hunter was not the best option, the mission he intended me to carry out against the government forces. It was a forced deal I had never accepted. A trap.

"There must be another way to save him," I whispered to myself.

I sat on the bed for half an hour or so. There were moments tears would suddenly rush through my eyes, and luckily, Commander Blake hadn't returned yet.

Certainly, there were updates on the rebels' whereabouts, and the special task force assigned by Tristan himself was bound to keep the information private.

Therefore, I needed to find someone who could trust me and disclose the details they'd gathered. Allen, perhaps?

But the commander had reassigned him to a new mission. Tristan was smart. Had he foreseen this? Maybe, he was thinking I was using his brother to spy on them or something. It came from his words, anyway. He'd said he didn't trust me at all. So, maybe that's how he perceived me. A spy against the government.

You're just overthinking, my subconscious thought.

As soon as I learned the location of the rebels, I'd go to the place myself and sneak out to save Phil without getting noticed by anyone. Anyway, who would suspect and even pay attention to the possibility that a woman like me, weak and fragile, would dare to go after him?

But where would I start? I was being taken away from this mission. The first thing I needed to do was work out how I could go back to camp with Commander Blake's permission. From there, I would take my purpose very seriously.

✶ ✶ ✶

It was getting dark already, and Tristan had finally returned later that afternoon, informing me that he'd roamed around the stores in town to purchase a set of clothes. At the same time, he said he'd ordered Morgan and his pal to go back to the camp for additional reinforcement.

"Why? Is there a problem?" I wondered, feeling a little anxious.

"Not really, just a preliminary precaution. The watchers claimed they've seen footprints around our safety zone. We're still investigating if it belongs to the locals or not," he answered.

Did he actually speak to me like a normal person?

"What?" he asked, sensing that I was little taken aback at his response.

"Nothing," I said, then I occupied the mini couch on the balcony and watched the sun take its final bow for the day.

"You look a little low today," he commented.

"If you were being taken away from your love, would you be happy?" I asked him, trying to initiate a conversation.

Tristan sighed; it was heavy and sad.

Oh, dear, I think you got him on the first try! my instinct cheered on.

"Do you really love my brother? Is he your boyfriend already?" he asked coldly, and it seemed like all the color in his face drained. This reaction stunned me; it was not the kind of thing I was trying to convey.

"No," I said, and his eyes lit up a little. "There is really nothing going on between us. When you saw us in the greenhouse, he admitted that he likes me. He is nice and sweet, but I only see him as a friend. I'm just trying to be nice to him because he is really a good man."

"By letting him kiss you? I don't believe it," he asked, sarcastic.

"It's not what you think it is," I interrupted, my voice raising a bit. "You just popped in at the wrong time, and you think we were doing something scandalous. I made it clear to him. I told him I was not interested in having a romantic affair, and he accepted it like a true gentleman. I guess, it was just some sort of, goodbye kiss or something," I explained and somehow, Tristan was starting to listen to my side.

"I see," he uttered, deeply contemplating. "But still, I am sending you back to the city. It is already final."

Oh. Shit.

I forced out a smile and nodded as if I had already accepted his decision. "Yeah, of course. It's just, it's my first love, actually. I still have no idea how I'm going to tell my mom. I mean, she knew how I waited for this mission and what I have been through just to qualify."

"So, when you said *your love*, you are referring to your career?" he asked, a little confused.

"Yes," I said and chuckled. "I told you, I don't have time for romance!"

Tristan let out a good laugh, which made him look ten years younger. It was the first time I'd heard him loosen up a bit, and it felt like he transformed into a new person overnight—or maybe this was how he acted whenever none of his troop was around? I wondered.

✳ ✳ ✳

I invited him for a bottle of beer to at least celebrate our unexpected truce. But of course, this was just an act to get his trust. I was not really fond of drinking alcohol, but this was the only way I knew to win his attention. I had to stay cautious. I had only two days left to make him change his mind. I had to return to the camp.

Finally, I was able to convince him. But for our safety, he suggested we should stay indoors and just request some beers from the room service.

Things were casual at first until we started to really have a great time. We ordered another bucket and drink, while we continued our heart to heart talk in the balcony, under the glow of the moonlight.

I could sense that Tristan was starting to relax as he got more comfortable being with me. I had caught him staring at me intently several times, and I could tell my plan was going to work.

But…Oh, dear.

Was I actually starting to admire him, too? Or was it just the effect of the alcohol? I tried to resist the temptation, but his dark, bewitching look was now consuming me. It turned me on, thinking that his eyes were actually fixed on mine alone. But then, the reality hit me. I had been longing to get this kind of attention from him from since from the start.

Why does he need to stare at me like that? I am melting.

Don't forget your plan, my mind reminded me as my heart started to get hooked at the unexpected twist.

I needed to fulfill my plan but… What was I doing? It was as if I was suddenly awakened. The dark, unfair plot that I created vanished from my head.

I should stop seducing him. I should go home and let the military do their job in rescuing my friend. But that wouldn't give me the assurance that they would actually succeed. Things might go the other way around. Hunter might even track and kill me for backing out.

Soon, I found myself trembling. The guilt and fear suddenly filled my senses, and I ended up crying in front of him. All I wanted was to stay, and it was such a shame to actually sell myself to him to get it. Worse, I was actually living up to the false accusation I'd fought against.

"Hey, what's wrong?" Tristan said, looking really concerned now.

"Why? Why are you so mean to me, Tristan?" I blurted out in tears. I was feeling dizzy, but I had to tell him how I felt in that moment or else I wouldn't get another chance to defend myself. I had to let him know I didn't deserve to be kicked out and humiliated like this. I had to let him know he didn't have the right to stain my reputation and tell the world that I was here to seduce his men.

And so, I spoke out, telling him all those things that I'd been keeping inside of me for a long time. But it pissed me off to see that he wasn't even feeling guilty about it at all. Instead, he put down the bottle of beer on the table and stood up, helping me to get on my feet.

"Let me take you to bed. You had too much drink already," he said.

But I pushed him away, determined to squeeze the answer out of him. It was now or never.

"Don't touch me! Just tell me what's your fucking problem with me! What have I done to you?! Why did you have to send me away and put me in this terrible mess?!" I cried hysterically, and he had to hold me tight in his strong arms to spare himself from my slaps.

"Aiya!" he said. "Calm down."

"I need to know! I have to know because it's fucking killing me inside, Tristan!" I mumbled, finally breaking down and giving in to him. I was like a tired candle losing its last wax to the fire that continued to consume it.

He held me in his arms tenderly, trying to soothe me. All I was left to do was cry, releasing all the pain, confusion and anger that had lived inside of me for months. He waited until my tears turned into gentle sobs. I was expecting him to respond angrily, but he mysteriously morphed into a compassionate being. His brown eyes were teary and full of remorse.

"I'm sorry," he said. "Believe me, I don't really understand myself. Would you believe me if I told you the real reason?"

I looked at him, my tears partly blinding my sight. "Why?" I whispered to him.

"I don't know how to express my emotion, the jealousy that I feel whenever you're being kind and close to other guys. You don't know how it feels… how it kills me to see you laughing with the others because I desperately want to share that moment with you alone… I want to know why you're smiling, or who makes you happy at that particular moment… I want to know the reason because I know in my heart I can even make you happier than that," Tristan said, his eyes and his voice trembling. It must have been quite difficult for a man like him to express and confess his deep emotion.

He wiped my tears away and tilted my chin gently, inviting me to look straight into his eyes.

"I love you, I desperately love you," he whispered, and his eyes were sad and gloomy. "But we're so apart… so apart I couldn't find a way to connect with you. To have time with you alone."

"T-Tristan… but… I thought…"

Tristan gently put his lips on mine. Unlike before, it was sweet and delicate. Full of love and hope. I searched for a reason to resist, but my mind was too tired to protest, and my heart was suddenly too powerful to reject the lovely feelings that he was suddenly offering.

This is what I want. I'm in love with Tristan Blake.

Soon, I found myself responding to his kisses. It tasted so good and fulfilling, and it was making us hunger and thirst even more. Then, he lifted me and carried me gently, his eyes smoldering my whole body as he laid me on the bed.

Slowly and gently, he climbed on top of me, returning to my lips as his hand explored my skin. I burned at each touch, making me pant and moan at the same time. It was so good… so gratifying…

"Please, make love to me tonight," he pleaded, his tone husky and hot.

I was too overwhelmed, I couldn't find my voice to assure him. So, I nodded and urged him to do more. This time, I wouldn't hold him off.

So, he continued to touch me, inch by inch, making sure it would make me feel so good. He pulled off my clothes, and I mirrored his action. Now, we were both admiring our naked bodies, determined to grasp the pleasure that both of us had been fighting off.

He went down in between my thighs and started licking me. His soft tongue tasted my juices, and I was left moaning at the strange and electrifying effect of his sweet and glorious assault.

Damn, it was so good. I arched my body as he inserted his finger gently inside.

"Oh," I mumbled. It hurt a lot, but at the same time, it felt wonderful. I had no idea that pain and pleasure could actually coexist in my body.

"Damn, you are so lovely," he whispered to me.

He moved back up, bit my ear and helped himself to my breast. He sucked me like a baby as his finger continued on my flower.

"Oh, please…" I pleaded, but I had really no idea what was I asking from him. I just wanted him to continue, but I was suddenly begging for a more strange and powerful feeling.

Tristan's dark and hungry face grinned wolfishly as if he knew exactly what I wanted.

He tore down his boxers, revealing his big and hard manhood.

Oh, I wondered how it would feel inside of me.

"I'm a virgin," I whispered to him, breathless.

So, he kissed me gently as if reassuring me that everything would be alright and once again, I nodded and gave in. He spread my legs apart and positioned himself in between them. For the last time, his hand touched my pussy as if preparing it for his intrusion. I took a deep breath and waited.

"This is going to hurt a bit, babe," he whispered to me.

"O-okay," I answered, both nervous and excited.

He kissed me one more time before he entered. "I will be gentle," he promised and before I knew it, I felt his painful and torturous entrance.

"Ah!" I cried, flinching. My body went numb, and Tristan patiently waited for me.

"Are you alright?" he asked, and his voice was already longing to dig deeper.

"Yes," I assured him. "I want it right now," I said.

Slowly… very cautiously… he moved in and out, allowing me to adjust. In no time, he was able to thrust at an average pace.

"Oh… Babe…" I heard him groan in satisfaction, rejoicing at the sensation.

"You're so delicious," he said and bit my lower lip harder as he continued.

It was so great and strange at the same time. But I liked it. I liked every bit of it, and to be honest, I knew that I'd do it over and over again just as long as it was with him.

Arching my body to his, Tristan plunged harder and deeper, and I was helplessly savoring the effect of his excruciating passion. The deeper he planted himself in me, the more I reached a feeling of satisfaction and pleasure that I never knew existed at all.

I couldn't believe I was surrendering myself to him and expecting nothing in return. I couldn't believe we'd ended up here, making love with each other for the first time.

CHAPTER 9

My body was sore when I woke up the next day. I was naked on the bed, and as I'd expected, Tristan was not with me anymore. Maybe he went out for another morning routine.

So, I remained on the bed, staring at the ceiling and imagining every detail of our lovemaking. What happened between us the night before was quite unforgettable. I strongly believed that it wasn't just a one-night stand.

He'd said he loved me. And I felt the same way, too.

Oh, you fell so easily, dear, be careful, my mind snapped in distaste.

In the middle of my daydream, I noticed the red spots on the bed. I'd forgotten I'd bled the night before. It had stained the sheet. So, I decided to get up, clean it and take a shower.

✶ ✶ ✶

Tristan came back, but I knew instantly that he had returned to his old self. Although he was not actually rude to me, the affection he'd shown me while we were on the bed had suddenly gone.

"Is everything alright?" I asked him, but he didn't even look at me.

"Get ready, we don't want to miss the train now," he muttered, and I froze on the spot immediately. *I thought we were good now.*

As we made our way to the train station with Tristan carrying my bag, I felt like my heart was ripping apart. I was so devastated and confused. He'd said he loved me. Why was he sending me away from him?

I looked away, quietly fighting the urge to let out my tears. Tristan wasn't meeting my gaze, and it was completely killing me inside. He was stiff and insensitive. He'd suddenly returned to the cold-hearted commander that I'd met before.

So, what had happened the previous night wasn't special after all. It was just nothing to him.

Looking down, I fought hard not to ask him about these things. Maybe, there was really nothing to talk about. He had just wanted to let off steam. He had just used and taken advantage of my body.

How reckless I had become! Why had I let this hard-hearted man claim my precious virginity?

Carrying my luggage with him, he went straight to the booth and purchased a ticket. Then, he escorted me to the waiting section and handed it to me. There were a lot of things I would have liked to ask him, but he wasn't even looking at me. He sat down beside me but he seemed very far away. It was quite tormenting. I didn't want to be apart from him. I didn't want to leave this way.

Finally, the train arrived. People started to fall in line to get in. To be honest, I was the last one who approached the queue, wondering why he was being so mean to me again.

"Goodbye," I muttered bitterly and looked away. That was all I could say. I waited for his response.

At last, his eyes met mine, but he didn't say anything. His thoughts seemed quite preoccupied. So, I gave up, kissed his lips gently instead for the last time and walked away, grabbing my trunk. It was the most painful thing that could ever happen to a woman who fell in love and lost her romance so quickly.

It was my turn now to enter the train. For the last time, I turned to where Tristan stood, hoping he was still there watching me go and making sure I would not escape.

To my dismay, he was already gone. Why was it so easy for him to lure and break someone's heart? Tears started to pour out from my eyes as the reality started to sink in my head. But before I could step into the train car, someone pulled me away abruptly.

"Don't go, stay with me," Tristan suddenly pleaded, his eyes anxious and at the same time hopeful.

"Tristan?" I said, sobbing. My heart suddenly beat hysterically.

"I can't let you go," he said and kissed me.

And it was as if I was in a fairy tale. I hugged him happily.

And soon, we found ourselves entwined with each other in the same room where we had spent the night together. It was cold outside, but we were burning with heat, indulging ourselves in the flame of love and unexpected romance that we had found in each other.

✶ ✶ ✶

He held me in his arms during the night. Though we were both exhausted, it felt like we were still not in the mood to sleep at all. Having him around made me feel alive, and I was certain I was having the same effect on him, as well.

"Are you sure you'll let me back in our volunteer mission?" I asked him, a little anxious at how I would explain the whole thing to my friends.

"Why? Are you having second thoughts now?" he said and chuckled amusedly.

"No, of course not," I said. "But what about the memo?" I asked, befuddled.

"Screw that memo," he said and kissed me on the forehead.

I smiled at him and snuggled against his chest. "Are we going to let them know about us?" I asked, though I knew it was quite a critical question.

"Not yet, babe," he said tenderly. "This is not the right time. Besides, it's going to ruin your career. I am not in the mood to send you back to the train station for the second time around."

I chuckled. "Don't worry about it. That's what I was going to suggest, anyway. Keep it private for a while."

Tristan sighed in relief. "Really? *Whew!* I thought you're going to slap my face again," he said mockingly.

"I'm just worried about Allen. It's going to break his heart if he finds out," I informed him. "Your brother is a good guy, you know."

"I couldn't agree more, babe. Don't worry, okay? I will take care of it and let him know at the perfect time. Besides, he won't be around the camp for a long time. I bet we'll be ready to inform him by the time he returns."

CHAPTER 10

Morgan and his pal George came back to the town early to pick up their commander. But as they parked in front of the travel lounge, they were obviously confused to find me still hanging around with their leader. Still, they kept the questions to themselves.

Were they really trained to keep their mouths shut unless they were told to speak? I wondered. Soldiers must have a great sense of self-control and patience for keeping things to themselves.

I climbed into the backseat as usual while Morgan held out the passenger's door for Tristan.

"No, you sit there. I'll take the backseat now. I wanted to rest, so you keep watch," he ordered immediately.

"Yes, sir," Morgan answered right away, looking confused.

So, Tristan sat beside me. He leaned back. Then, he put on his sunglasses, used his jacket as a blanket and pretended to be asleep. I could sense Morgan and George's confounded glances in the rearview mirror along the way, but I chose not to give them a hint of what was happening at all.

Finally, their suspicious gazes returned to their real duty, keeping an eye on the road. Then, all of a sudden Tristan took my hand and put it underneath his jacket.

"I want to hold you," he whispered quietly.

Then, slowly, his hand secretly reached for my legs as he guided my hand to his torso. He was hard already. My heart raced at the thrill.

I spread my legs apart discreetly and saw the wild and dark grin on his face. My skirt would give him easy access. Meanwhile, his other hand let go of my mine as he unzipped his pants carefully. Then, he went back to leading my hand to his cock. I massaged him and watched his face as he kept himself silent.

I heaved a deep sigh, fighting hard not to moan when I felt his finger moving to my clit. I bit my free hand and pretended I was looking at the scenery through the window. Luckily, none of his men took notice of our naughty action. I was wet and needy. I wanted him inside of me at that moment, but I had to keep still. I closed my eyes, savouring his movements as I continued to stroke him. And after a moment or so, just like me, he was close, I knew.

Suddenly, I noticed a cargo truck in front of our vehicle and let out a moan at the same time it blew its horn at the drivers in its way. I exploded in pleasure. No one noticed my release, except for Tristan.

✶ ✶ ✶

We arrived at the camp early in the afternoon, and everyone was shocked to see me, getting out of the vehicle and heading back to the medical team station. But before we could walk through half of the open field, Riane was rushing to meet me halfway. She was squealing in happiness, completely making a scene, catching everybody else's attention.

"Oh, my god! Aiya! You're back!" she shouted until she finally embraced me tightly. "I can't believe it! Why? How?"

I glanced at Tristan, and he was feigning his cold facial expression. "I'll see you around, Miss Shaw," he said, playfully putting his fingers to his lips. I bit my lip, fighting hard not to smile at the thought of how that hand had touched me. He smirked and eventually left me with my friend, who was still confused and surprised.

I watched him walk away and head straight to his office, which was just a few steps away. Riane, on the other hand, looked a little anxious.

"Did he give you a hard time?" she asked, worried. She knew how harsh he was to me, and I couldn't blame her for asking. We had been together for three days, and she must be wondering how the hell I survived his company.

"No, not really. We're cool," I assured her.

"Oh," she said. "He looked relaxed, though. I just find it hard to believe." Then, she helped me with my luggage and escorted me back to the dormitory.

Meanwhile, Sandra was already waiting for me at the entrance, all too pleased to welcome me back again.

"I'm so happy you're back!" she exclaimed and hugged me tightly. "I knew Commander Blake still had the heart to listen and weigh things up!"

"Yeah," was all I could reply. "Thanks for always backing me up," I added.

Sandra flustered. "Oh, that's nothing. Defending you to Commander Blake was the least I could do. When I spoke to him the night before you left, I thought he wasn't interested. But see? Heaven always listens! It knew you were innocent."

So, she did speak to him then.

"I agree," I replied and hugged her. "Thank you."

Riane gazed at the two of us affectionately. I never knew I was that important to them. Somehow, a twinge of guilt struck my chest. These two ladies needed to know my real score with him.

Not today, dear, my subconscious reminded me.

"You can rest for today, by the way," Sandra said kindly. "You've been on a long journey. You must be really tired."

Yeah, I am. But not for the reason you think,

"Oh, really? Thanks a lot, I really appreciate it," I answered. She was right. I felt exhausted, and my body was still sore—but it was not because of the long journey.

I grinned secretly as I remembered the wonderful time I'd had with him.

✷ ✷ ✷

I hadn't seen Tristan the whole day, and although I missed him, I was okay. He had been gone for days; there were certainly a lot of errands he had to catch up on. After all, he was always busy even before this. It was just fair to let him do his job. Sooner or later, I knew he would come after me.

Hmm… I wonder how he will do that?

I dozed off in bed feeling relieved. Finally, I was convinced that I didn't have to stress myself out about Phil's captivity. As Tristan had mentioned last night when I'd asked him about the case, there was really nothing to worry about. He assured me that Allen was taking care of it and he could not wait to see them coming back to the camp with my friend. Although he didn't tell me all the details of their plans, I trusted that they were not taking it for granted like how they skillfully rescued us before.

The thing was, was it still necessary to tell him about the forced "deal" I had with Hunter? I mean, it wasn't like I'd do it. But I was worried it would turn him off and that he'd accuse me and be cruel again. Besides, I didn't want to be on their watchlist. He might doubt my loyalty then.

You should be honest with each other, my heart whispered, and I knew it was right.

Fine, I would tell him tomorrow and surrender the substance to him. But this would mean relating the incident of Joe Black's breaking in. I was scared of the mood it might create. But I knew I had to do it and along the way assure him that I would never, ever comply with the enemy's scheme. He loved me, and for sure, he trusted me, too.

✶ ✶ ✶

I was on my way to the clinic to report for duty when suddenly, someone grabbed my arm in the corridor, dragging me to a secluded corner of the aisle.

"Good morning, babe," Tristan greeted me excitedly.

"Tristan, oh! You'll give me a heart attack!" I scolded him, but my heart beat happily upon seeing him.

"Sorry I scared you," he said and chuckled. Then he wrapped me in his arms and granted me a sweet kiss. "What's your plan today?" he asked.

"Err… work? Of course, I'll stay in the clinic. I have a duty to fulfill. So do you," I answered, my tone a little sarcastic.

"Of course," he said. "What a stupid question. I'll take a round in the clinic and see you, okay? So, stay there and wait for me," he instructed very carefully as if it would be a sin to disobey his instruction.

"Okay," I said. He kissed me once more and pecked my neck.

"I miss you already," he whispered in my ear in the most seductive way.

"I miss you, too," I replied, returning his kisses.

His eyes roamed all over my features. Then, he playfully unbuttoned the top of my blouse and gazed at me darkly. As he cupped my breasts quickly and touched my nipples, he kissed my neck delicately once more, making me moan in silence. It was sweet torture; I was already so into him.

Tristan smirked, and finally, he let go. He gave me one more smack on the lips and fixed my blouse.

"I'll see you later," he whispered and composed himself, too. He was already breathing heavily, and I could tell he was hard.

"Okay," I said, a little disoriented.

Well, that had been really unexpected... and hot. I'd never thought he could be that carefree and playful. It was like he became a totally different person now. I tried to focus on my job even if it was quite difficult. Things felt odd, considering I was having a secret affair with the commander. I had to mentally slap my face to maintain my efficiency.

"Feeling better now?" I asked Zoey, who collapsed in the middle of their field training.

She was brought to the clinic a few hours before. Thankfully, it was really nothing serious. It turned out she was just having dysmenorrhea, a period-related condition.

"Yes, thanks a lot for that," she answered sincerely. "You know, the boys will never understand the feeling."

"You're right," I agreed, laughing with her. "But I recommend you skip the training today. Your body must be so exhausted, it's begging for some rest."

Zoey pouted. "Can you give me a pain reliever instead? It's embarrassing. How would I'd explain this to the Commander. I'd rather make it through the day than speak to him and excuse myself."

Damn. Tristan must be so hard on them.

"Really?" I asked in disbelief.

Rolling her eyes, Zoey nodded. "Yeah. Men and women here are always treated equally. So, we are expected to perform and do the stuff we're supposed to do regardless of the condition of our hormones."

"That's terrible," I muttered.

"Well, it's okay. I chose this path anyway. So, I must endure the consequences. You know, no pain, no gain," she replied, grinning.

I agreed with her once again. But as her assigned medical advisor, it was my duty to take care of her welfare.

"That very inspiring, Zoey," I told her. "But you're staying in your barracks for today, and that's final. If you have trouble with the commander, I'll speak with him personally and discuss this matter with him."

She looked as if she could not believe her ears, but she smiled at me appreciatively.

"You're the first medical personnel who would do that," she commented.

"Do what?" I wondered all of a sudden.

"Well, discussing severe cramps with the commander," she answered, quite amused. "You don't really have to, you know. But

I appreciate it. It's just, I don't think he'll find this issue necessary to consume his time."

Oh, dear. You have no idea what I could do to him, I thought to myself.

✶ ✶ ✶

I insisted that Zoey stay at the barracks for the day and rest. Although she was a little hesitant, she obliged, as I promised I'd talk to Tristan about it.

Well, of course, I didn't want to bypass their platoon leader, so I decided to speak to him first and foremost, hoping it would be enough. So, I left the clinic for a while and found out, he was in the meeting room with Tristan.

I waited in front of the closed door. If they were in the middle of an important meeting, I thought, this was not the best time to intervene.

So, after a few more minutes I decided to leave. Tristan would be in the clinic at lunch anyway; I'd just speak to him about it later. But as soon as I stepped away, Tristan and his men went out of the door, catching me.

"Miss Shaw," he called out. "What are you doing here?" He raised an eyebrow as if I was caught in the middle of wrongdoing.

"C-commander Blake," I murmured. Looking around, all eyes were on me now, probably waiting for another confrontation between us. Everybody knew how their leader used to treat me. "I came here to have a word with Lieutenant Tomas," I said, blushing.

All eyes turned to the lieutenant as if he was guilty of something while Tristan raised an eyebrow; even more, his eyes were jealous and a bit disappointed. Was he expecting me to say I was there for him?

106

Perhaps. *Who knows, right?*

So, I cleared my throat to clarify the matter immediately. Tristan was very jealous in nature. I didn't want him to think I was interested in other men.

"How can I help you, Miss Shaw?" Lieutenant Tomas asked, looking a bit embarrassed at the scorching look of his colleagues, which made me feel a little uncomfortable. So, they decided to give us some privacy, except for Tristan who seemed very upset.

"Well, actually." I looked at both of them. "If you have a minute, this may also concern you, Commander Blake," I said, trying to make it up to him. And I was right; he wanted to be involved.

So, he invited us to step into the room instead. Lieutenant Tomas shrugged his shoulders but didn't dare to protest. As soon as we were inside, I informed them immediately that it wasn't really that urgent.

I explained why I demanded Zoey to skip the training for the day. If she didn't feel better, I suggested to extend it until tomorrow. Well, of course, I updated my diagnosis and Lieutenant Tomas sneered as if he couldn't believe why this was worth their time. No wonder Zoey felt that way.

I felt so offended. I took a deep breath and controlled my emotions. It was obvious men would never understand the pain of this condition.

"If that's really necessary, let her take a break then, lieutenant. After all, we are all humans and not robots," Tristan said, and immediately, Tomas stopped laughing. He suddenly became confused. He could not believe his Commander was really on my side for the first time.

He cleared his throat, switching the decision he had in mind. "Very well then, Miss Shaw," he said. "You know better than me with regards to that."

I glanced at my love, who was standing behind him, and he winked at me, smiling treacherously at the same time. It was as if he was telling me I owed him something and he was expecting a payback later.

I could not believe it would be so easy to get permission. So, I excitedly dropped by at the barracks to tell my patient not to worry now, and Zoey could not believe it either.

"Ugh! Thank you so much, Miss Aiyana," she said in gratitude, finally lying flat on her bed. "I can rest well now."

"No worries," I said happily.

✶ ✶ ✶

As promised, Tristan visited the clinic at lunchtime. But since Sandra was also around, he actually behaved himself. Lunch was also served in our office for the first time, which I found a bit odd. But because our head nurse claimed it was an annual routine by the Commander to inspect and audit the medical department, I assumed it was part of the custom, too.

I remained as casual as possible while Sandra patiently reported all the facts to Tristan. Meanwhile, Morgan, who was always beside him, could not help but eye me suspiciously, and I had to double my effort not to show him a hint of my real score with his boss.

It was very hard to swallow my food, thinking that even if he was acting like the usual commander of the base, his desire to have me at that moment was completely evident in the way he would stare at me.

What if he snatched me again, pulled me into a corner, and then we got caught by somebody? It would be a huge disaster! Zoey had mentioned how I was already drawing the attention of the female troops, and I didn't want to add fuel to the fire at all.

"You seem a bit off, Miss Shaw," Tristan commented, diverting my attention. "What's troubling you?"

Sandra turned to me anxiously. I presumed she was worried that a new tension between us may have arisen.

"I'm sorry, sir," I answered, not meeting his eyes because I was already melting. I had to come up with an alibi quickly, and my thoughts didn't fail me. "I'm just wondering… is there any update about Phil?"

There was a moment of silence. A part of me felt regretful for bringing up the subject, but I hoped Tristan would not find the question offensive.

Morgan cleared his throat, breaking the awkward silence while Sandra pretended she was busy drinking the water in her glass.

Meanwhile, Tristan remained calm and composed. "I'm glad you reminded me, Miss Shaw," he said. "I actually included this subject on our agenda today."

I sighed in relief, along with Sandra and Morgan. It was obvious on their faces that they never saw that one coming.

Tristan continued. "I just had Allen's report. They spotted Joe Black and some of the rebels on the north side of the mountain, and he sent some of his men to follow them. It won't take long until we can finally find their new hideout."

Sandra gasped, her eyes a bit teary. "Oh, that's great news! Phil will be joining us soon!" she exclaimed happily.

I must admit I felt overwhelmed and happy. I trusted them. I was confident that they could manage to rescue Phil soon and bring him back to us safely. Furthermore, there was no need for me to fulfill the deal in exchange for his freedom.

The thought made me cry silent tears. I shouldn't have let myself be troubled with that stupid deal before. I should have confided in the rescue team from the start.

But will you still tell him about it? My mind asked out of nowhere.

✶ ✶ ✶

I was waiting for Riane and Lily to take over my post. In a few minutes now, Sandra and I would be off duty, and it would be their turn to stay in the clinic for the next shift.

The Commander's visit and the meeting were adjourned late in the afternoon, giving us more time to relax.

"Have you noticed?" Sandra asked all of a sudden while we were cleaning up.

"Noticed what?" I asked curiously.

"It's Commander Blake. Is he terminally ill or something?" she wondered and grinned like she was playing a private joke in her head.

"What?? I don't think so. He seems really in good shape. What made you ask, anyway?" I asked her seriously. Was she seeing symptoms on him that I hadn't noticed?

Sandra laughed loudly. "Loosen up, I'm just kidding," she said, amused at my reaction. "I'm saying, I just notice his behavior changed all of a sudden especially at how he is treating you. Don't tell me you're not aware of it."

"Oh, that!" I mumbled, thinking of what was best to say. "Yeah, I think he's behaving now a bit."

Then, Sandra stopped and turned to me, her eyes were scrutinizing. "What happened back there?"

"What do you mean?" I asked her, my face turning red now, so I

110

had to keep moving and pretend to be busy with my stuff so she wouldn't notice it.

"Why did he suddenly cancel your memo? And he obviously became nicer to you these past few days," she said.

"I-I am not sure," I lied. "We just had a serious talk when we were left on the mainland. I explained and justified myself to him. Maybe, I just got lucky. He seemed to be in a good mood. So, maybe that's the reason why he gave me a second chance."

Even before Sandra could respond, Morgan knocked on the door, and Sandra went to answer it.

"Miss Shaw," he said after he nodded and greeted my head nurse. "Commander Blake wants to have a word with you. Do you have a minute?"

"Oh, okay. I'll be clocking out in ten minutes," I informed him.

"No, it's okay," Sandra interrupted. "Off you go now, I'll just wait for Lily and Riane."

✷ ✷ ✷

I stepped into Tristan's office, expecting to see him sitting on his office chair. The memory of his grumpy mood when he abruptly planned to take me here gave me a chill. It was still frightening.

"Tristan?" I called.

"Hey, babe," he answered from behind the door, and I was caught off guard, almost stumbling on my feet.

"There you are again!" I complained, feeling really annoyed. "You scare the hell out of me! Don't ever do that again!" I playfully slapped his cheek.

"I'm sorry," he laughed and wrapped his arms around me. He kissed me sweetly and caressed my face. "How's your day? You looked a little tense the whole afternoon."

"Who wouldn't feel tense? Imagine having the Commander personally checking your work," I answered, rolling my eyes. "And I think Morgan knows something about us."

"Don't worry about him," he assured me. Then, he effortlessly carried me and sat me on his desk. "You shouldn't feel uncomfortable around me. You should not see me as your Commander. I'm your lover," he continued and tucked my hair behind my ears.

I smiled and planted my lips on his. I could not ask for more. I couldn't believe he was really mine.

"Okay, I'll keep that in mind," I said and giggled.

Tristan looked into my eyes tenderly, alluring me again. He walked away for a second and reached for the door, making sure it was locked.

And in no time, he was kissing me again.

✳ ✳ ✳

It was late in the evening when suddenly I woke up from my deep sleep. I stared blankly at the ceiling, feeling strange and sensing something was wrong.

And then, it caught my attention. There was a shadow of a man outside the window of our dormitory, and I was pretty sure it had been there for a long time now, probably waiting and observing.

I got up and took a look since my bed was closer. Joe Black was outside, and he was patiently waiting for me to notice his presence.

"Great instinct you have in there, Miss Shaw," he murmured.

"Stop bothering me," I said, keeping my voice low.

"Meet me at the greenhouse now," he ordered, his voice menacing.

112

He held out a grenade, threatening to throw it inside the room if I refused to follow his instruction.

✱ ✱ ✱

"Hunter is asking for an update," Joe said as soon as I found him in the greenhouse. "He thinks you're taking your time for too long now. Are you backing out?"

"I never agreed on that," I said. "I don't want to do it. I am not killing innocent people just to fulfill your agenda."

"Oh, so you think that will work now? Whether you agreed or not, you have a deal, and Hunter is not fond of people who do not honor their word," he threatened, circling me like a dangerous animal.

I pulled out the small bottle from my pocket, returning it to him.

"I didn't promise anything to him," I insisted, fighting hard not to tremble in front of him even if fear was starting to consume me like a wildfire.

"Come on, Miss Shaw," he said. "What's so hard about mixing the poison with their meal? You wouldn't even get the blame for that because you're not the cook."

"Tell him I don't kill people. And please, give this back to him," I replied.

"No, keep it," Joe ordered, his voice firm and authoritative. "You have a week to do as planned, and if you fail, we will cut off Phil's head and send it to you. Then, who knows what we might do next? Maybe we'll do the same thing to yours. We have somebody inside the camp closely monitoring you. You can't run from us, Miss Shaw."

He left without a backward glance, and I stood there for a while, trembling and speechless. The cold wind was blowing my hair, but I could not find the strength to savor the calmness of the breeze. I was filled with terror.

Did he just say there was a traitor inside the camp?

The rebels were really serious about this thing, and indeed, there was a no way out. Either I would accomplish the mission, or I would wait for Phil's death and my own.

Hence, I had no choice but to tell Tristan everything before it was too late. Maybe, this threat would push the team to expedite their rescue mission. The best thing I could do now was to accept the possibility of losing his love and trust again after my confession.

Yes, this action might kill my heart and even take my own life, too. But at least the military would be saved from a mass grave, the cook will be spared from being accused of a hideous crime, and Phil might be rescued.

Maybe, I was born to sacrifice. Maybe, I was destined to die this way. It was now time to stop thinking about my welfare to save a great number.

CHAPTER 11

The thought kept haunting me until the next day. I needed to speak to Tristan before it was too late. So, before reporting for duty, I headed straight to his office, hoping he was not yet busy.

But it was still locked from outside. Obviously, he had not been there yet. *Where is he? He used to be here early ahead of everybody.*

I walked through the corridor and searched for him in the field. He was not there either, and I was running out of time. I had to be in the clinic within ten minutes.

So, I canceled the plan temporarily, but still, I vowed that as soon as I got the chance, I would spill the beans and prepare myself for the outcome. For sure, I would become subject to a lot of questioning procedures and countless interrogations. By then, my innocence would be compromised again. I might lose Tristan's love and trust, and that was scaring me the most.

Riane greeted me as soon as I came in. She was packing her stuff, waiting for me to take over the post.

"There you are. You're five minutes late," she said, glancing at her wristwatch.

"Sorry, I got a little distracted," I answered sheepishly.

115

Riane chuckled and tapped me on the shoulder. "It's alright. I can't blame you. Allen hasn't been around for a while. You guys must have missed each other a lot."

"What do you mean?" I asked, confounded.

Rolling her eyes, Riane paused for a while and turned to me. "Haven't you heard? Allen is back. He and some of the soldiers had just arrived early this morning."

"Oh, really?" I gasped, excitedly.

"Yeah, I thought you had an early coffee or something because you're late," she explained.

"No, we haven't seen each other yet," I answered defensively. So, maybe that was why Tristan was not around.

"Okay," Riane said. "That's only my presumption. Allen came here early looking for you. So, I thought you'd met already."

I thought I should refrain seeing him from now on and that made me a little sad. He was my good friend and companion.

But that's the best thing to do, my subconscious reassured me.

Although I missed the long conversations with Allen, I didn't want his brother to get upset. Tristan was a jealous person. We were both aware of how Allen felt about me.

Have they talked about it already while I was asleep? I wondered. *I hope so.*

Tristan mentioned he would handle it once Allen came back.

There was nothing much to do for the day. In fact, Sandra spent the time decorating the clinic just to keep herself busy.

"Looks like you have a visitor," Sandra informed me, grinning in my direction.

When I looked up, Allen was standing at the door. It looked like he'd lost some weight, but he was still as neat and as handsome as I remembered.

"Hey," I said as I saw the stem of middlemist in his hand.

"Hey, there sleeping beauty!" he greeted happily. "It's nice to see you again."

Sandra giggled and decided to leave us alone. "I'll just go and check our supplies," she said, obviously making it up. I knew we'd just finished the inventory before the commander's annual visit, and there was no need to do it again this soon.

"How are you?" Allen asked sweetly. "I picked this on our way back," he said, handing the flower to me.

"I'm good, thanks," I answered and accepted it. Was he aware of everything that had happened? Did he know about the memo? Was he aware that his brother tried to kick me out? What about my affair with him?

I guessed that it hadn't come to his attention yet because he was still here, trying to win my heart again.

"How's your mission? Is Phil okay?" I asked, worried that he had brought bad news with him because they had come back unexpectedly.

"Don't worry about him," he said, trying not to divulge more information. "Sooner or later, he'll join us here."

"But when?" I asked again, my voice demanding an answer.

Allen sighed patiently and took his seat on one of the chairs beside me. "You know how confidential it is, Aiya," he told me kindly. "But I assure you, we're almost there."

"Okay," I said, a little disappointed.

"I came here to talk to you and catch up. It's been a while. I missed you," he said, and his honesty was something I couldn't bear to hear. Tristan should have informed him about us beforehand. I wasn't ready to deal with that myself.

My mood changed, and I knew he felt it, too.

"Is there something wrong?" he asked, anxious.

"Listen, Allen. I don't think we should see each other again like this," I said, sadly.

"What do you mean?" he said, incredulous. There was a sudden jolt of disenchantment in his tone, as if his light had instantly died out. "Is it because of the issue we had in the greenhouse? Did Tristan give you a hard time?"

So, he knew about it.

"It is not like that," I answered. How was I supposed to confess the truth about me and his brother? This was quite difficult. I didn't want to hurt him. I'd told him before I was not ready for romance, yet here I was, unexpectedly having a secret affair with the commander.

Allen cut me off; he was not in the mood anymore. His face was so upset, and for the first time, it worried me. I had never seen him so distressed like this.

"I know you can't love me back, but I thought you were giving me a chance to show it? I mean, I just came back from a mission. I'm so excited to see you," he said, but he was now serious, and he seemed angry.

"I'm sorry, Allen," I said, feeling guilty. "I didn't mean to upset you."

He didn't say a word for a moment. "Well, at least, you should have waited a few more days before you decided to dump me. It's not really a very nice way to welcome me back." Allen stood up. "So, I guess I should go now," he added and walked out the door without another word.

Unlike before, he didn't look back and didn't even bother to grant me his kind and sweet usual smile. Well, what should I expect? I broke his heart just like that. It must be quite annoying. I didn't like the idea, but I shouldn't have given him false hope from the start.

I would just leave it all to Tristan now. I would like to believe that sooner or later, he would understand why I was doing this, and I was confident that he was bold enough to accept it… that I was in love with his brother.

✳ ✳ ✳

Finally, I got the chance to speak with Tristan alone in the meeting room. As usual, I waited a few more minutes before his men left the hall. They must have discussed a lot of things. Half of the military population in the camp had attended the session and of course, Allen was present too.

"How long have you been there hiding?" Tristan asked amusedly as soon as I appeared at the secluded corner.

"For a while," I answered, sneaking quickly inside the room. "I need to talk to you."

Tristan closed the door, planting a sweet kiss on my lips. He hugged me and sighed. He seemed tired but still, his eyes lit up a bit when he stared at me.

"I'm sorry, I was so busy the whole day," he apologized sincerely.

"It's alright," I answered, kissing him back. "Have you talked to Allen about us yet? He visited me this morning, and it ended up not going so well. I think he's upset."

Tristan heaved a deep breath. Obviously, they hadn't talked about it. "I'm sorry, we never got the chance. We're busy with the rescue mission. Honestly, we never expected them to arrive this morning."

"I see," I said. "It's okay, don't rush." It looked like they were in some kind of emergency situation.

"I'd be honest with you, babe," he whispered. "Last night, Allen's troop caught Joe Black, and it looked like he was making his way out of our camp. They got Hunter, too, along the way because he tried to save him. We're convinced they have an ally here inside. They have a spy mingling with us, and we need to find out who it is immediately."

I froze on the spot. So, they caught Joe after he spoke to me in the greenhouse? They also cornered Hunter in the area! Had he said something about me? I suddenly felt scared for my safety.

"Joe managed to escape, but we're sure they will come back for their leader soon, so we'd better get prepared," he continued. "We still have Hunter, though. There would be a great chance we could finally rescue your friend."

"H-hasn't he confessed yet who the spy was?" I wondered, feeling nervous now. What if he pointed to me?

"No," Tristan said. "He keeps telling us to just wait and see."

I was completely shaken, and Tristan noticed my reaction. How would I tell him Joe Black had come here and spoken to me?

"Don't worry, babe. We got this under control, okay? So, please, stop worrying. We're here to protect you all, and I'm here to protect you," he whispered, gently caressing my face.

I hugged him tightly. I was more scared of losing his love and trust for me if he found out the truth about the deal. I guessed telling him I was not intending to do it anyway would be useless.

He would definitely not believe it.

All of a sudden, the door busted open and Allen caught us in each other's arms. His face turned red in fury as he realized what was going on.

"So, now you're after my brother," he said, speaking directly to me. "Indeed, you're very skilled at seducing men."

"Allen, don't speak to her like that. She's my girlfriend now," Tristan said, his tone offended and threatening. He angled me behind him as if shielding me from unseen force from his brother.

Allen sneered in disgust. "Fuck!" he exclaimed. "Are you fucking serious? Come on, Commander Tristan! You can do better than that! She is just using you! She's tricking us all!"

"What the hell are you talking about?" Tristan asked furiously.

I was trembling. *Allen certainly knows the truth now. But how?*

"We checked out the surveillance camera right after our meeting. And it turns out that the innocent-playing woman behind you was the rebel's spy. She was recorded talking to Joe Black in the greenhouse last night!" he exclaimed.

Tristan was shocked. He turned to me, his face in disbelief. "Is this true?" he asked. "Did you talk to Joe Black?"

"It's not what you think it is," I answered, my tears suddenly pouring out in fear.

"Then what?! If you're not spying on us, why would Joe Black keep coming back in the camp to speak with you?!!" he grunted, his face stiff and disappointed.

"No wonder she keeps asking about our plan with Phil's rescue," Allen added, completely disgusted.

"No!" I said. "You're wrong! He's my friend, and I'm worried about him!"

"Yeah, right," Allen replied, and all the kindness, all the sweet smiles he reserved just for me had gone too soon. "Do you actually believe we'll buy that? You're busted already, Miss Shaw. You can't fool us anymore. How careless of you to think that we wouldn't bother setting up a camera in the greenhouse."

"No, I am not one of them! Please, Tristan… please believe me…" I pleaded, clinging to his arm like a baby. "Joe Black was threatening me. They're forcing me to poison you all in exchange for Phil's release. If I won't comply, they will kill him and they will kill me, too."

I was shaking as I accounted for the terror that ran through my whole being as I heard such a threat from him.

"Damn, Aiya," Tristan shook his head, and I could not figure out if he was in doubt of me or not. He looked away, gritting his teeth while Allen remained standing near the door, waiting for his brother's final order.

"You have to believe me," I cried. "This is the reason why I came here today. I've been looking for you since this morning to tell you everything about it."

"Come on, stop playing around," Allen interrupted.

Tristan stared at the window as if trying to make up his mind. He seemed confused, but I didn't think he would believe me. But still, I had to try my best to keep his confidence in me as I told the truth.

"It's true!" I cried, leaning on the long table for support now. I felt like I was going to pass out. Tristan's silence was quite a torture at that moment.

Finally, Tristan turned to me, his eyes serious and disappointed. "You had every chance to tell me before, Aiya. Now, give me a good and valid reason why would I still trust and believe you?" he said.

"Because you're the only one I have right now. I didn't obey the rebels, and that's why they're after me. I'm scared for my friend, and I fear for my life right now. And I need you… I need you… you said you would protect me," I mumbled, breaking down.

I knew it was too much to expect his arms around me at the moment. All I was hoping was his love and trust for me wouldn't disappear.

CHAPTER 12

All of a sudden, the siren rang loudly around the base, leaving our discussion unfinished.

George busted through the door with a gun in his hand. "Sir, we've been attacked! The rebels are here!" he said sharply.

Soon enough, there were gunshots everywhere. Tristan and Allen reached for their weapons immediately, and I was left startled and confused. It looked like everyone had forgotten I was there.

"Go and alert everyone! Bring the other personnel to the safe house!" Tristan ordered.

So, as soon as they were gone, I ran to reach the safe house where some of us were supposed to be hiding during an emergency crisis like this, but Allen grabbed my arm furiously, and Tristan did nothing but look away.

"Not so fast, Miss Shaw!" Allen said angrily, dragging me to the corner. "Stay here! Don't even think to run away!" he ordered and joined the battle.

Little did we know, Joe Black was behind me, and before I could shout for help or fight back, he punched me in the stomach so hard I passed out.

✳ ✳ ✳

My whole body was aching and bruised as I woke to find my wrists tied with a rope that stretched around a large tree like a captured animal. I was hungry and sick, and my fever was not helping at all to keep myself calm and composed.

Though nobody dared to sexually assault me, the physical torture was nothing compared to the realization that the rebels were able to free their master again from the hands of the military.

I wondered what had happened back in the military base. Was everybody safe? Were they able to save Phil in the middle of the attack? I cried weakly. I couldn't even find the strength to get on my feet. I was on the ground, filthy and cramped in pain like a torn flower ready to be disposed of.

"Forget about that fat man. We got the girl, anyway," said a voice behind the bushes, but I couldn't figure out who it was or how many of them were talking. I was too weak to turn around. I closed my aching eyes and listened instead. My sense of hearing was the only strong sense that remained in me.

I supposed they were having a small celebration. I could hear them drinking and singing, laughing and rejoicing. It was dark, and I had no idea how long I'd been there or what time or even what day it is.

Then, there were footsteps coming.

"What's up, Morgan?" I heard Hunter's voice in the background. "Do you have good news for us?"

Morgan? I was hoping it was not the Morgan I knew.

"Negative," the familiar voice answered.

Oh, my god! It was really Morgan! He is the spy!

"We can't use her to lure Tristan anymore. They believe she's one of us and she just escaped with you. He doesn't care about her at all. In fact, she is considered a criminal now," Morgan continued.

I heard Hunter throw something in frustration. "We should move out now then, we're not safe here," he said after a while.

"What about Miss Shaw? Are we still bringing her?" Joe's voice asked, curious.

"She's useless now. Better cut her head off before we leave at dawn. But before that, I'll have some fun with her," he added maliciously, and they laughed loudly at the idea.

✶ ✶ ✶

When I woke up again, I had a glimmer of hope I would be rescued, just as Phil had successfully made it through the dark days he'd spent in the hands of the enemies. But finding out Tristan and the others thought I really was a spy, all the remaining hope in me was gone.

Oh, Tristan… I cried.

For the first time, I realized I would rather die. Knowing that my love hated me and that he disregarded his promise to protect me, there was no sense in believing he would come right now to save me.

I cried hopelessly as I waited for my final hours. Was Hunter serious about having me after their celebration? And tomorrow, before dawn, they would end my life, and my untold story would be buried in the ground with me. I had already explained myself to him, but he chose to believe the lies more than the affection that I had shown him, and that was breaking my heart the most.

How could he say he loves me, yet he could not even believe a single word that I've said?

My heart was torn, my whole soul completely devastated. Even if I was spared from this punishment, how would I even live again and move on thinking that Tristan did not choose me after all? I had to learn to live my life without him.

I leaned on the tree trunk and stayed like that for a long time. As if I was already dead, I was tempted to stop myself from breathing. Sooner or later, the rebels would come and behead me, anyway. What was the point of waiting in agony? The pain that my heart felt in that moment was worse than my aching and tortured body.

It was such a shame that it was only my mother who would cry for my death. The rest of the country would believe that I deserved it because I'd betrayed the government.

In the midst of my anguish, I heard a faint sound of approaching footsteps.

They're finished… it's my time now… Goodbye, Tristan…

Hunter was eyeing me wildly. "Well, I guess you're still meant for me," he said, licking his lower lip and staring at me as if I were his next meal.

I looked away, too weak to respond. He came near, and I felt his breath as he whispered in my ear.

"It'll be fun, honey," he said, and moved my hair out of my face.

Hunter ripped off my blouse, and I cried out loudly, desperately seeking someone's help.

"Please…" I mumbled, tears streaming from my eyes.

"Hmmm…" he murmured, licking my neck.

"NO! Please!!!!" I yelled in protest, but I knew it was hopeless. Still, I fought hard, and he was enraged. He punched me in the stomach and the world went black for a moment.

When I came to my senses, I was expecting to find my body naked and abused. I cried silently, my eyes closed, ready to welcome my bitter fate.

It was nearly dawn. They would behead me soon.

I imagined the eternal darkness that awaited me.

But there was complete silence.

Am I dead?

Then, a gentle hand touched my face, caressing my tormented skin where blood, dirt, tears and bruises were smeared together.

"Babe…" whispered the voice I had been longing to hear.

"Babe, can you hear me?" the voice called again.

I opened my eyes, half wondering if I was just hallucinating. "T-Tristan? You came," I uttered weakly, not even recognizing my own voice. Suddenly, my heart beat again, sending its life through every vein in my body.

He put his finger over his lips, instructing me not to catch somebody's attention from the nearby group, who were still having a good time while Hunter was lying motionless on the ground. It was then I realized Tristan had stopped the attack. I was okay.

"What have they done to you?" he whispered in remorse, touching my bruised body.

I nestled my head in his arms and cried silent tears; the depths of pain were starting to flare up. I had to control myself from howling. But it was a mixture of fear, joy and relief.

"I-I thought you weren't coming," I mumbled, still crying.

Tristan was regretful and furious. "I'm sorry, babe," he said and planted a kiss on my lips and forehead, trying to console me, reassuring me that no one could hurt me anymore.

He pulled out a pocket knife and freed my hands cautiously. He rubbed my contused wrists and kissed them, too, the pain and remorse in his eyes evident.

"They're going to pay for this," he muttered angrily.

✷ ✷ ✷

The commotion started as another battle arose. In the middle of the otherwise silent evening in the woods, the sounds of gunshots and brawling men were overpowering the soft breeze coming from the leaves and branches of enormous trees around.

"Hold on to me," Tristan said, lifting me. "I'll take you away from here."

But out of nowhere, Hunter was awake, with Tristan's weapon in his hand. It was pointing towards us, so Tristan put me down carefully and secretly pulled out his gun.

"WHAT DID YOU DO TO HER?!" he shouted furiously.

Hunter barked a laugh, his gun pointing at Tristan's chest.

It happened so fast, I could not figure out how they ended up brawling against each other, rolling here and there on the ground, punching and pushing each other until their faces were cut and bleeding.

"Tristan!" I called as if it could help him in that moment.

How the hell I could help him?

I was too weak to attack. I saw Tristan's gun fly into the air and land just a few inches away from me. Taking advantage of the opportunity, I crawled toward it, trying to reach it as fast as I could manage.

But then, Hunter stepped on my hand.

"Not so fast, honey," he mumbled, panting and sneering.

Tristan was down beside me. He didn't seem quite defeated, but he was defenseless. Hunter got the weapon from the ground, then he pointed it directly at my love.

"Finally," Hunter uttered in triumph.

BANG! BANG! BANG!

"NO!!!" I howled. I shut my eyes. There was silence. A few seconds of tormenting silence. Then, a body hit the ground. I was frightened to open my eyes and see Tristan bathed in his own blood.

But then...

"Allen!" It was Tristan's voice bringing me back to reality. So, I opened my eyes once more, and hope glimmered like a new sprout of seed in spring. My heart jumped with joy as I found Hunter's lifeless body instead.

"Hey there, bro!" Allen responded, winking and grinning proudly at us. "Guess I just arrived in time."

"Oh, thank God! " I mumbled in relief. Allen was able to shoot Hunter and save his brother from death. It was all over.

"Let's go and bring her back home," Allen suggested.

"Yeah... yeah..." was all Tristan could answer.

He stood up and reached for me happily, but even before I felt his lips on mine, I lost consciousness and passed out in his arms.

✦ **CHAPTER 13** ✦

The war was finally over. The fall of the rebels' leader, Hunter, had led hundreds of enemies surrendering themselves to the government. Sylvania Mountain has finally achieved peace, and the civilians' fear of battle and gunshots were just a part of history.

Who would have believed that I still had a bright future after all of this chaos? I was spared from accusation and judgment through Tristan and Allen's help.

Although it was difficult at first for Tristan to convince his brother of my innocence, still he came around in the end. It turned out they'd kept the files to themselves and didn't even drag my name into it.

"We knew Morgan was the spy," Tristan explained when I told him about what I heard from Morgan back in the enemies' hideout. "So, we had to lure him. We had to make him believe that we hated you, and we wouldn't come to rescue you to confuse their team."

"So, you mean you'd been watching them there overnight?" I asked.

"Yeah, he'd been under surveillance already. We knew one day he'd sneaked out and would report to Hunter. Then, it happened. We followed him that night and were ready to attack. But of course, we just had to wait for the perfect timing," he clarified.

✳ ✳ ✳

I could not contain the happiness I felt as I walked down the aisle, wearing my beautiful wedding dress and holding the bouquet of white roses in my hands.

It was like a dream. Something that I never imagined I would experience.

The once rude, cold-hearted Commander Tristan Blake was standing at the end of the red carpet, waiting, staring and smiling at me with his teary-eyed face.

It seemed he could not wait to marry me, either.

"You're so beautiful, babe," he whispered in adoration when we finally met in front of our close friends and relatives.

He was so gorgeous, I wanted to kiss him already. I knew he loved me more than anyone. More than his power, medals and awards, he'd risked his position just to come and save me, and that was enough reason to believe that he would take care of me and protect me no matter what happened.

"And you look so handsome yourself, my love," I replied, fighting the urge to kiss him too soon.

"Well, it was all because I have to keep up with you," he replied sweetly and planted a kiss on my hand.

"Enough with the seducing looks and touches," Riane interrupted as she pointed out the presence of the minister waiting in front of us.

Looking around, everybody giggled, including the President himself, who had, to our surprise, accepted an invitation. Embarrassed, Tristan raised his hand as if he was caught in the middle of mischief.

"Oh, I'm sorry! My bad," he said, chuckling.

✳ ✳ ✳

"...And now, I would like to present to you... Mr. and Mrs. Tristan Blake!"

There were loud cheers and roars among the crowd when finally, Tristan claimed his first kiss as my husband.

Our colleagues back in the war zone didn't miss the chance to witness our matrimony, including my very much safe and alive friend Phil. Of course, Lily and Sandra were there, too.

Meanwhile, Tristan's brother and best man was standing behind him. I noticed he was smiling, too, but his attention was on my friend and maid of honor, Riane. Yes, they'd been dating for a few months, and I couldn't be more thrilled and happy for both of them. I knew Riane had had an eye for Allen since the start of our deployment, and Allen deserved to be loved wholeheartedly.

At our wedding party, everyone around shared their thoughts and good wishes for us.

The captain took advantage of the time to congratulate Tristan, Allen and their whole team for bringing back the peace at the mountain. In fact, he mentioned that they had been promoted.

"But we shall discuss the details soon, not here! We don't want to delay the honeymoon," he said, chuckling, and everyone around laughed with him.

Finally, he proposed a toast, and the crowd enthusiastically joined us.

"May I have this dance?" Tristan whispered when all the guests seemed busy.

I blushed at his sudden invitation. We hadn't danced before.

"Since when did you became fond of dancing like this?" I asked him as soon as we occupied the floor.

"Well, I always wanted to do this with you before, but there was really no opportunity. Besides, there was no good music on the mountain," he answered, grinning.

"Well, that sounds a bit romantic," I admitted and giggled in amusement.

Indeed, he was not the same man I had met. His cold and frozen heart had finally melted. It was now beating for me… just for me…

"I wish the party would end soon; I can't wait to have you in bed," he murmured seductively. Instantly, all the butterflies in my stomach felt alive.

"Me, too," I said, biting his ear lightly.

"Hmmm…" he whispered. "Don't test my patience," he warned.

He looked around the dance floor, and we realized more than half of the crowd was dancing and having a good time now, their attention finally diverted.

"It's time!" Tristan confided in a low voice. He bit my earlobe and then swiftly dragged me away behind the curtain, pulling me towards the exit.

"Are you serious? We can't sneak out!" I insisted, laughing.

Tristan carried me playfully and without an effort.

"Yes, we can, honey!" he answered proudly.

We ran away from the party, excitedly heading towards the nearby five-star hotel we'd booked. Soon enough, we were in the majestic room, filled with red rose petals scattered on the floor. Tristan put me down and started to unzip my dress, his eyes dark and alluring.

"Ready?" he asked with a wolfish grin.

I smiled and helped him undress me, guiding his hand on my skin like never before.

I couldn't wait to feel him inside me again. I still couldn't believe we really belonged to each other now. He was mine and I his.

Certainly, I would do everything to not let his heart be cold again.

THE END

AMAZON REVIEW

WHAT DID YOU THINK OF "COLD HEARTED"?

Thank you for purchasing this book! If you enjoyed reading "Cold Hearted", I'd love to hear your feedback and hope that you could leave a review on Amazon. Your feedback is very crucial for a newly self-published author like myself and will help me improve future projects. I look forward to reading your reviews!

Please click on the link below, which will take you directly to the book's review page.

Amazon book review link: http://www.amazon.com/review/create-review?&asin=B08574S4DD

www.ingramcontent.com/pod-product-compliance
Lightning Source LLC
Chambersburg PA
CBHW030331160726
47992CB00005B/2238